Beldon stepped toward her and she backed away, her derriere hitting the wall. There was nowhere else to go.

Her chin went up in defiance. "I will *not* be intimidated."

But she wasn't immune to being other things she feared. Her pulse raced at his nearness. At this distance he was far more intoxicating than he'd ever been on the dance floor. The atmosphere between them had changed during the altercation, pregnant now with expectation. Something explosive and potent was brewing, about to brim over.

A wicked glint lit his eyes. "I don't mean to intimidate you, Lilya. I mean to kiss you."

* * *

Secret Life of a Scandalous Debutante
Harlequin® Historical #1058—September 2011

Author Note

Beldon and Lilya's adventure is set against the interesting backdrop of the Greek struggle for independence. The London conference seemed too good to pass up. The Phanariots are a fascinating group of people, and a large population of them did indeed move to London after the Chios massacre in 1822. They lived predominantly in the area of Finsbury Circus, which even today bears the imprint of Greek tradition. All those things in the story are true. However, there are some embellished fictions in the story, too.

In the eastern part of Europe, secret societies abounded during that time. The Filiki Eteria is one of the most well-known. However, the Filiki Adamao is entirely a product of my imagination. The other embellished fiction is the presence of the diamond. Pink diamonds like Lilya's Adamao are considered rare even today.

I hope you enjoy Beldon and Lilya's quest, which is as much an adventure to protect the diamond as it is a journey of self-discovery. Through their diamond quest they come to truly know themselves and open themselves up to the endless possibilities of love.

Please stop by my website at www.Bronwynnscott.com, or my blog at www.Bronwynswriting.blogspot.com, and say hi! I love hearing from readers.

BRONWYN SCOTT

SECRET LIFE OF A SCANDALOUS DEBUTANTE

TORONTO NEW YORK LONDON
AMSTERDAM PARIS SYDNEY HAMBURG
STOCKHOLM ATHENS TOKYO MILAN MADRID
PRAGUE WARSAW BUDAPEST AUCKLAND

Recycling programs
for this product may
not exist in your area.

ISBN-13: 978-0-373-29658-3

SECRET LIFE OF A SCANDALOUS DEBUTANTE

Copyright © 2011 by Nikki Poppen

www.Harlequin.com

Printed in U.S.A.

For adventurers everywhere who are not afraid to
embrace a new and uncertain future
even when it takes them away from everything they know.

For my editor, Lucy Gilmour,
to celebrate our first book together.
May it be the beginning of an exciting new journey.

Chapter One

Beldon Stratten, the fourth Baron Pendennys, was on a mission of matrimonial importance. His affairs were in order: the one prequisite needed for a good marriage or a good death among London's social elite. Having been neither married nor dead, he'd have to take their word for it. There were those among his acquaintances who argued there wasn't much difference between the two. *He* would reserve judgement.

His gaze roved the room, quartering it with purpose. He would choose one of *them*. Perhaps the lovely Miss Canby with her modest fortune, but impeccable bloodlines; maybe Miss Ellsworthy, granddaughter of a viscount, whose financial endowment made up for the lack of other endowments; or the elegant Elizabeth Smithbridge with her icy beauty and twenty thousand pounds. Beldon gave a mental shrug. No. Not Miss Smithbridge. Too cold. A man must have his standards, it wasn't *all* about the money.

Dear Lord, did Miss Canby just wink at him? She waltzed by with the young heir to an earldom, clearly hedging her bets. That was definitely a wink.

Beldon grabbed up a chilled flute of champagne from a passing footman and silently toasted himself.

Welcome to the Season.

Four months of sizing up the opportunities.

And four months of being sized up. He was no naïve young blood first come to town. While he was assessing the available women, admittedly some more available than others, they were assessing him.

Beldon sipped from the flute. Lady Eleanor Braithmore floated by in a froth of white lace and pink ribbons, daughter of an earl and the most eligible heiress of the Season. All his common sense, and he had a healthy dose of it, suggested he make his suit in that direction. Wealthy, young and pretty, Eleanor was all a well-bred gentleman should desire.

Until his gaze moved on and he saw *her*.

More precisely, until he saw her *back*.

The *her* in question was not Eleanor Braithmore. In fact, he didn't know who she was.

The woman was stunning.

Granted, he could only see her back, but what a back. Beldon gave silent thanks to the fashion gods who'd decreed that this year's gowns be low, off-the-shoulder creations that revealed a tantalising glimpse of a woman's back and the feminine swell of a neatly rounded shoulder.

The woman in question wore the latest style exceptionally well. Her raven-dark hair was piled high and threaded with lengths of pearls, exposing the delicate column of her neck and enough of her back to cause a jolt of desire to fire straight to his core. He was suddenly and exceedingly aware of himself as a sexual being, a man in tune with his natural urges. What he could do with a woman like that! The very sight of her begged a man to conjure fantasies.

He closed his eyes for a moment, imagining the feel of that straight, elegant back beneath the caress of his fingertips. Even now, across the room and her face unseen, his fingers itched to skim the sensual surface of her skin, his lips lightly brushing the place where neck met shoulders.

He seduced her in his mind. She would be exquisite by candlelight. He would approach her from behind, settle his hands, light but firm, on those bare shoulders and push the delicate material of her gown down the length of her arms, letting it glide over the slim flare of her hips, until the whole of her back was revealed; the indentation at the small where it gave way to the curved globes of her derrière.

She would be superb nude.

A man knew these things instinctively. *And a smart man banished 'those things' to the recesses of his mind where they belonged, unable to interfere with logic and rational thought.*

Beldon Stratten was nothing if not a smart man.

There was a time and place for such indulgences and in the past, he'd indulged rather frequently under those circumstances. Now was not the time. He was here for a wife, not an affair with a delicious stranger.

Beldon drew a deep breath and relinquished the fantasy. Whoever she was, she wasn't on his mental list of candidates and for obviously good reasons. A temptress-wife brought a whole dowry of potential complications with her. He believed firmly in the adage, all things in moderation. A life of excesses was a life beyond control. His father's lack of it had taught him that.

Then the woman turned, her face fully revealed and all his good intentions hit the well-paved road to hell.

His step slowed.

His breath hitched.

Lilya.

His mystery woman was no mystery at all. Instead, she was none other than Lilya Stefanov, his friend Valerian's ward. He'd met her before at Valerian's home in Cornwall, but not recently. This past year his investments had taken him often from home.

The transformation was astonishing. She bore little resemblance to the neat but plainly dressed girl he recalled. In his absence, she'd become a woman of extraordinary beauty. Tonight she was turned out to perfection in a crêpe gown of creamy ivory. Where other girls appeared washed out by the pristine whiteness of their gowns, Lilya positively glowed, managing to look ethereal amid the Season's preference for heavy silks. She looked like a woman; a confident female in a ballroom full of girls fresh from the schoolroom who hadn't so much as touched a man's sleeve before tonight. There was no inherent reticence about Lilya. It was evident in her gaze. A certain spark burned in those beautiful sloe eyes of hers, a spark that held all nature of exotic promise.

With a bachelor's eye for all things lovely and female, Beldon noted she was surrounded by beaux. Who would not want to bask in the rays of her beauty? She'd have half of London at her feet in no time. But he would not be one of them, unlooked-for visceral urges aside.

She was not what he considered a top candidate for himself. He knew what he wanted. He'd spent the winter contemplating the ideal wife: a woman who had the experience to run an estate, a woman who brought a certain financial security to the marriage. He'd spent ten years making the Pendennys holdings respectable again. He'd prefer his wife have the ability to continue that.

Aside from her loveliness, Lilya met neither of his two conditions. She was Valerian's ward, a refugee Phanariot from Macedonia; her abilities to fully integrate into English society were dubious and untried. Her hostessing skills merely masked his larger concern. Even if those skills should prove exemplary, there was the financial barrier. She had Valerian's generous dowry. However, Beldon could not bring himself to take his friend's money. Scruples aside, the fact still remained that he needed to marry for money, at least a little of it. He could not afford the luxury of a poor marriage.

And yet she was somehow irresistible. He should at least go and make his presence known. Duty compelled it of him as Valerian's friend and brother-in-law. Everyone would think it odd if he didn't greet her. He would go over and say hello, nothing more, and then get back to the pursuit of Eleanor Braithmore, the perfect English rose.

The perfectly handsome man was staring at her with intense blue eyes reminiscent of hot coals, studying, searing. It was the 'searing' part that had caught Lilya's attention.

No, he was no longer staring, he was moving. Towards her with a purpose in his stride that left no doubt of his destination.

She did not recognise him at first, although there was a slight sense of familiarity about him: the broad shoulders, the height, the confident walk of a man who knew what he was about, and the chestnut hair. In the end, it was the eyes that tipped his hand—strikingly blue and intense as he neared. She only knew one man with eyes like that.

Beldon Stratten.

So he was back.

Her mind assimilated the information objectively. Her stomach fluttered, assimilating the information in an entirely different way that had nothing to do with his return and everything to do with the way he was bent over her hand, all refined grace and male potency combined together in dark evening wear.

'*Enchanté*, Miss Stefanov. It has been a long time.'

'Lord Pendennys, how charming to see you.' Lilya dipped a modest curtsy, reminding herself of reality. As Valerian's brother-in-law he was obligated to acknowledge her. A sillier girl than she might have swooned. As it was, she was far too conscious of the blue gaze holding her own, of the unexpected *frisson* of excitement his most proper touch elicited. He'd done nothing wrong, yet he'd managed to turn a perfunctory greeting into something more.

Perhaps that was why women were gazing not so discreetly over the edges of their fans at him. A quick scan of the area indicated he was becoming an item of interest. Why not? A confident man was an attractive man and he had confidence in spades.

Such a reaction made her wonder what other

mysterious skills Beldon Stratten might possess in order to evoke that level of feminine attention. It was a short journey down the path to another curious thought; if a simple touch affected her so thoroughly, what else might he evoke? A delicious shiver trembled through her at the idea.

Beldon deftly caught up the dance card dangling from her wrist and discovered the upcoming waltz was available, the only one left empty. 'I would like to claim a dance. I hope I am not too late.'

It was immediately clear that he embodied a higher calibre of man than the usual young bloods surrounding her. Here was a man in his prime; a man old enough to assume responsibility, but young enough to thoroughly enjoy the pleasures of life.

What those pleasures might be, Lilya could only guess. He was not a man given to the obvious *ton*nish excesses of gambling and womanising. For all his confidence, it was also apparent from the formality of his manners that Beldon Stratten was a man of controlled reserve. He emanated an aura of power restrained, a certain air of mysterious reserve. If one could just get behind those eyes and see into that mind, one might see great secrets, one might unleash something primal, Lilya suspected. But for now, he remained something of an impenetrable fortress.

That man wanted to dance with her.

Now.

Another flutter swept her in anticipation. She felt

like a green girl next to this polished man and all of his town bronze.

'Are you nervous, Miss Stefanov?' he asked, his voice low and private at her ear as he guided them to an empty place on the floor. 'I would not have expected it from you.'

'Nervous' wasn't the right word for what she was feeling but how to describe the thrill his simplest touch conjured? 'It is just that I have not seen you in a long while.'

'And I you, Miss Stefanov. When I saw you, you nearly stalled me in my tracks.'

Lord, the man flattered with exquisite expertise. She nearly believed him. Perhaps if his eyes had been warmer, she might have. But while his gaze remained intent, it was also aloof.

The music started. Beldon's hand rested lightly at her waist, firm and possessive, pushing her awareness of him to new heights. 'Shall we, Miss Stefanov? You do not strike me as a woman given to nerves over a dance.'

'Do you know me so well, then, after a few minutes' acquaintance?' she parried. He might be Valerian's brother-in-law but, she'd never shared a private conversation with him. For all intents and purposes, he was a stranger, albeit a stranger she'd fancied from afar; handsome and bold, he was the stuff of heroes. If she was smart, that's where she'd keep him, too. A man like this was dangerous. She could indulge in the fantasy of a single waltz, but that was all. If she indulged in more, she'd likely end up with a broken heart or worse. No, Beldon Stratten was not for her.

Lilya put her hand up to his shoulder, alert to the intimate proximity of the dance. He surrounded her subtly; the sandalwood and citrus of his cologne teased her nostrils; the flex of his muscles flirted with her fingertips through layers of glove and fabric, reminding her of the absolute maleness of him; a reminder that was intoxicating and more than a little unsettling. She might just prove his suppositions wrong.

She had danced with men before, been held like this before, and not once had she experienced this extreme awareness of a partner.

He moved them into the dance with consummate ease, oblivious to his growing effect on her. Perhaps he affected all women this way. Lilya fell in with his smooth execution of the steps, finding comfort in the familiarity of the patterns. Then she made her first mistake.

She should have kept her eyes affixed on some invisible point over his shoulder as protocol demanded, but the temptation to study this man proved too great. She tipped her head up to look at his face and instantly knew it to be a grave misstep. It did nothing to quell his appeal.

The attraction and mystery of him were indelibly etched together in his features, in the intelligent but remote blue eyes, in the sharp, clean lines of his jaw and the mouth that so rarely gave over to a smile. It was a handsome, but not accessible, face. This was not a man one casually approached. This was a man who decided whom he would approach and when, which made it all the more exciting that he'd approached her.

Everything about Beldon Stratten bespoke purpose, an intriguing departure from some of the other men she'd danced with; older men whose boredom with their station was written in the angles of their faces; younger men who hadn't any idea of what they might become, no calling evident to them. But here was a man who knew who he was and what he wanted. That knowledge made him interesting, made him magnetic. Maybe that was why women looked at him over the tips of their fans.

'Are you enjoying yourself tonight?' Beldon asked, sweeping them through the turn at the top of the ballroom.

'Of course, everything is so grand in London, one cannot help but love the balls.'

'I noticed Lord Idlefield is on your card later. May I be so bold as to warn you he will live up to his name?'

Lilya nearly missed the joke. She had not expected humour from this man. She caught the reference just in time and smiled broadly in response, her intrigue with him ratcheting up another notch. She cocked her head in a coquettish challenge, daring him to continue along this vein. 'And Lord Fairborough? I am to dance a cotillion with him after supper.'

Beldon arched a chestnut brow in doubting question. 'He aspires to be a breeder of sheep, ewe know.'

Lilya laughed and the rarest of things occurred. Beldon Stratten's mouth turned up into a smile that took the whole of his face, transforming all the purpose etched there into lines of merriment. For a brief instant they were co-conspirators in jollity, laughing together over their joke.

The dance ended, taking with it his smile and the fleeting magic that had stirred between them. Beldon returned her to her court, every fibre of him once again the polite, aloof gentleman. Cinderella must have felt this way when the clock struck midnight

'Thank you for the dance, Miss Stefanov. I cannot recall when I've enjoyed waltzing more.' He bent over her hand again, this time in farewell. 'It is no wonder you're besieged with admirers—you are truly a diamond of the first water.'

A diamond of the first water.

Lilya stiffened at the comment. She knew what the phrase meant. It was used to describe a young woman of the highest refinements and beauty, a virtuous model beyond reproach. But to Lilya diamonds would always represent something much darker.

'Then we must dance again soon.' She mustered a light laugh.

But not too soon, she thought, watching him retreat. She was astute enough to know Beldon Stratten held the ability to be a hazardous distraction for her. Her reaction to him this evening was proof enough. She could not give in to whatever adventure he might offer.

It was for his good as well as her own. She knew what no one else did: she was not an ordinary débutante. No matter how many beaux she collected or how much money Valerian endowed her with, she was not one of them, not really. The other débutantes carried their pedigrees and dowries with them like calling cards. They'd been bred for this just as she'd been bred to be the keeper of a secret; she held in her possession the Phanar Diamond, a jewel that could change the fate of nations.

Chapter Two

That night she dreamt of her home in Negush. She would rather have dreamt of Beldon Stratten and their dance. Instead, it was her father's face she saw, his eyes bright, his voice low as he whispered the Stefanov legacy.

Whoever possesses the diamond possesses the power to finance a nation. There is no other jewel like it on earth. It is the rarest of rarities. In the hands of the right man it might become a tool for greatness. In the hands of the wrong man, it would become a weapon of tyranny. Who is to say who that man might be or what he might become? For that reason, the diamond has been secretly entrusted to us. It is up to us to see that no one possesses it. The risk is too great. This was the charge given to the

Stefanovs four hundred years ago in Constantino-
ple, and it is the same charge we continue today...

Lilya bolted upright in bed clammy with sweat,
her breathing coming fast and hard. She'd been
dreaming of the last terrible days before the upris-
ing. Her family had been there, all of them; her
brother Alexei, her aunt Natasha, baby Constantine,
and her father.

Lilya's breathing returned to its normal pace and
she squinted against the invasion of bright light.
She'd fallen asleep with the curtains open. It was
morning and from the looks of it, the morning was
well advanced.

Her stomach rumbled, confirming that she'd slept
through her usual breakfast hour. She reached for
the hand pull to call for a cup of hot chocolate. But
she'd no more than reached for the pull when a knock
sounded at her door.

'Come in.' Lilya fell back against the pillows,
resigned to a rumbling stomach. It would be too
much to hope for that her maid would be that efficient.

Philippa stood there, dressed for driving, a sharp
contrast to her own nightgown. 'Good, you're up.
Beldon's here and he has invited us to ride in the
park.' Philippa smiled warmly and wagged a finger
at her, taking a seat at the foot of the bed. 'You didn't
tell me Beldon was there last night, and that you'd

danced.' Philippa had stayed home from the ball pleading a headache the last minute.

Lilya turned her attentions to her wardrobe, hoping her face didn't give her away. 'He did his duty. He was very polite and it was considerate of him to think of me.' The last thing she needed was Philippa playing matchmaker. Coming up to London for the Season had been an excellent excuse to be in town while the peace talks over Greek Independence were going on. She'd felt compelled out of loyalty to her father and the family charge to be on hand for the occasion for which they'd fought and died. But it was becoming harder than she'd expected to avoid potential entanglements. It seemed everyone was in town for two reasons: marriage or politics, and some were here for both.

'Beldon plans to marry this Season,' Philippa announced.

Ah, suspicions confirmed. Everyone *was* in town for two reasons. Even Beldon was here for marriage. She hoped he wouldn't marry too soon. The thought of him devoted to another was oddly deflating.

Lilya shrugged into her gown, trying not to think of Beldon married. It would be to someone else, of course. She certainly wasn't marrying anyone. She could not ask anyone to share the burden of the diamond. Her father had tried to do both. He'd had a family while protecting the diamond. He ended up dead and most of his family with him. She would not make the same mistake and drag anyone into the covert dangers of her life.

She turned her back and let Philippa do up her buttons.

'Personally, I think he's going to choose Lady Eleanor.' Philippa gave the buttons a final pat to signal she was finished. 'Perhaps that's the reason he's so keen on riding in the park today. It's usually a bit too tame for him.'

'Lady Eleanor Braithmore?' Lilya asked, somewhat surprised that the smooth-faced Lady Eleanor would garner the attentions of a man of Beldon's depths. She snatched up a bonnet, tamping down a ridiculous stab of disappointment. What would a virile man like Beldon want with a girl who had the personality of a milquetoast?

'Does that displease you?'

Lilya shrugged, unwilling to say anything disparaging. 'No, Lady Eleanor's a lovely girl. It's just happened so quickly, I suppose.'

'Beldon is not a man to remain idle once his mind is set on a goal. Don't worry, it will happen for you, too, just wait and see. We'll find you someone to marry. Now, as to that, has anyone snared your attentions? You've been surrounded by so many, surely one has stood out.'

Lilya kept her response vague. 'No one yet, though many are pleasant.' She could no more say 'yes' than she could say 'no'. The only man of note was inappropriate. She couldn't very well say Beldon.

'Perhaps the marquis's son will be riding in the park,' Philippa continued, handing her a pair of gloves. 'He's twenty-eight and well situated even before he inherits. I noticed he has been avid in his attentions. Val knows his father. If you would encourage him just the slightest, I think he'd come up to scratch.'

'Yes, I will consider him especially...*to avoid most assiduously*,' Lilya murmured, buttoning up her jacket. What a disaster it would be if she became a marchioness. Any marriage was unthinkable for the risk it posed, but marriage to a high-ranking peer would be the worst. Her life would become excessively public. She'd be written about in society columns and it would be all that much easier for someone to find her.

Assuming that was the kind of marriage she wanted. In all honesty, the diamond protected her from thinking whether or not an English marriage would suit her. In truth she did not think an English marriage would fit her temperament. The English girls she'd met and many of the young wives, too, were insipid creatures with no temerity of their own. They were utterly their husbands' property right down to the opinions they possessed. She had never lived like that and she did not believe she was capable of it, certainly not for a man.

* * *

Philippa's intuition was correct. They did encounter Lady Eleanor Braithmore in the park, sitting demurely in a white landau twirling a frothy confection of a parasol. Beldon was all dashing solicitude, paying compliments to her beauty from atop his bay hunter, bareheaded in the sun, so strikingly handsome, the very picture of English manhood, that Lilya had to remind herself to breathe.

Did the girl understand the import of his attentions? Surely she must. As an earl's daughter, she'd been raised to make a match like the one Beldon would offer her.

Lilya sighed against a tender remembrance of long ago. She'd tried love foolishly once, before she'd understood the depth of her father's mistakes. At sixteen, she'd had attentions such as the ones Beldon lavished on Eleanor Braithmore. The result had been disaster. The young man, an importer's promising son, had died. She'd learned from the tragedy of that single indulgence. She must remain alone.

She told herself she did not begrudge Lady Eleanor Beldon's specific attentions, just the sentiment behind them. Such a courtship would never be hers with anyone again.

A trio of gentlemen approached their carriages where they were pulled over on the verge, drawing Lilya's attention away from Beldon's courtship efforts.

'Pendennys, it is good to see you,' one of the young men called out. Lilya recognised him vaguely as being Lady Eleanor's brother, a cocky young blood of twenty-two. She thought she saw Beldon cringe slightly at the young man's familiarity, but the expression was quickly concealed.

'Bandon, it's good to see you.' Beldon's jaw tightened with annoyance, affirming her thought earlier that Beldon was not a man to be approached casually.

'I'd like you to meet some of my friends. This is Lord Crawford and this is Mr Agyros, who is in town for the London talks. M'father is involved with those, of course,' young Lord Bandon puffed with his borrowed self-importance.

The introductions were made and Lilya was conscious of Mr Agyros's eyes on her at regular intervals while the others talked. He was a handsome man and she blushed a little under the intense scrutiny of his mysterious dark eyes.

'You must excuse my impertinence, Miss Stefanov. I can't help but wonder about your name. It has a Russian sound to it and yet your accent, slight as it is, sounds like home to me. Is there any chance you're from the Balkan regions or the Phanar itself?' He flashed a wide, flattering smile and Lilya found herself smiling back in spite of her regular penchant for caution.

'Where is home for you, Mr Agyros?' she asked

politely, thinking it best to counter a question with a question until she knew more. She'd learned to be vigilant on both fronts, direct and indirect danger. Direct danger operated under the assumption that someone knew she was in London and she had the diamond. Indirect danger operated under the premise that it only took one person to recognise her and pass that information on even inadvertently to dangerous sources.

In Cornwall at Val's country estate, there'd been little chance of encountering anyone from the Balkan region. But London, during peace talks, was far more perilous. Danger could lurk in multiple guises. It was time to start wearing a knife beneath her gowns again.

He smiled once more and said fondly, 'Constantinople by way of my uncle's business in Marseilles these days.'

Lilya relaxed a little, trying to balance a very real danger against a very real paranoia. 'Are you here long?'

Mr Agyros was probably harmless, a diplomatic aide looking to see the world and perhaps use this opportunity to gain some status back home. This meeting in the park seemed far too random to be anything other than coincidence. Still, her conscience warned, there was the indirect danger. He might tell someone...

Mr Agyros gave an elegant shrug. 'It will depend

on the negotiations.' Then he offered her another disarming smile. 'I'll be here long enough to attend the Latimore rout. May I hope you'll be in attendance as well? I find I cannot take my eyes off you, as unseemly as it is.' They laughed at the joke; the Latimore rout was tomorrow evening.

Perhaps she was more homesick than she cared to admit or perhaps thinking of the diamond had stirred emotions and contradictions within her best left alone. Maybe this once she could indulge in conversation, nothing more, with a man from her part of the world, who'd seen the places she'd seen and walked the streets she'd walked. Lilya found herself saying, 'I would love nothing better.'

His eyes twinkled. The dark-haired Adonis on horseback gave her a short bow from his horse and another of his wide, ready smiles, a very different face than Beldon's. The others, sensing the conversation was at an end, made their farewells and wheeled their horses around, taking Lady Eleanor and her landau with them. Lilya watched the group go, acutely aware that Beldon studied her with curiosity.

Beldon edged his horse next to hers. 'Isn't it enough that you've gathered all the gentlemen in England to your banner, but now you must steal the hearts of all of Europe?'

He'd been listening. She wasn't sure what to make of it. 'Should I be flattered or offended that you were eavesdropping?'

'Eavesdropping doesn't count in public,' he countered easily, refusing to rise to the bait. 'Your trick won't work twice, you know. Unlike Mr Agyros, I will not be distracted by a question. You never did answer him. Why didn't you tell him where you're from?'

She hadn't really thought it would work twice either, but a girl had to try. Lilya offered a vague truth. 'I like to be sure of people before I tell them too much.'

'I thought you would have been delighted to see someone from your corner of the world,' Beldon pushed.

If at first you don't succeed, try, try again, and this time with a smile for variation. Lilya fixed him with a coy smile. 'Hasn't anyone told you a gentleman doesn't press a lady for more answers than she wants to give?'

Foiled again. Beldon stayed the course of conversation.

'I wonder what that says of our Mr Agyros? He seemed quite interested in whatever you had to say.' Beldon's tone was sharp, almost defensive, as if he was eager to point out that he hadn't been the only one guilty of a misstep.

Lilya raised her eyebrows. 'That is precisely my point.' She lowered her voice to confidential tones in hopes of putting an end to his enquiry. 'If I am reticent to disclose personal information, it is my business.'

He nodded. His eyes were upon her, solemn and considering. For a moment, they might have been the only two people in the bustling, crowded park. The power of him, the leashed control that she'd perceived last night, was palpable today.

'My apologies, Miss Stefanov. I thought simply of how lonely it is for you. England must seem a lifetime away from your homeland.' He was unerringly polite in his deference, his face a bland mask of gentlemanly propriety, yet, like last night, he stirred her unexpectedly. Last night it had been his touch. Today, it was his words.

A tear threatened in her eye and she quickly looked away. Lilya was moved by the kind direction of Beldon's thoughts. It was interesting to discover how others might view her interactions with her countrymen. Where she saw danger, they saw offers of companionship. But Lilya could not partake in those perceptions. The moment she set aside her awareness was the moment she'd likely be dead. It was a testimony to the irony of fate that in order to protect her countrymen she was cut off from them entirely. In turn, she suspected them, feared them for the dangers they might pose to her. Constant fear was tiring and there was sadness in knowing she could not go back to those warmer climes, to the arms of her extended family.

'My home is here. Val and Philippa are my family now,' Lilya said simply.

'And me, too. I hope you consider me family as well,' Beldon added.

'Of course,' Lilya amended hastily. 'But you'll be starting your own family soon and your life will be even less centred around your sister's.' They were bold words from an unmarried girl. Unmarried girls did not speak to eligible bachelors about their matrimonial plans. But it was a good way to establish distance between her and Beldon. She was family, after all. He'd said so himself. Let him regret the remark if he didn't like the permissions it gave her.

From the tight set of his jaw, she could see he didn't.

'Yes, wedding bells are in my future' was all he said before kicking his horse into motion and returning to the path.

What was wrong with him? A day ago, that pronouncement would have flooded him with satisfaction; another goal achieved, another step forwards for the Pendennys legacy. He had decided on his most likely choices. All that remained was deciding who it would be, something he could accomplish within a month.

He'd need a few weeks for dancing, for drives in the park and other social avenues to get to know the women in question before making an official offer.

It would likely be Miss Braithmore. He would not be rejected. He'd danced with her later last night and she'd been amenable to his conversation, staring up at him with dark brown eyes. He would be the one to win the heiress. He could not have hoped of such a match a few years ago.

The prospect did not fill him with the usual contentment and he laid the reasons for it at Lilya's door. Last night she'd been a potent and uncharacteristic distraction for his customary good sense. She'd been vibrant and alive in a ballroom full of pattern-card girls. There was nothing wrong with the pattern card, he reminded himself. It was a template of virtuous womanhood. The pattern card just wasn't very exciting.

Lilya was exciting.

There was a level of wit to her conversation and her lively eyes suggested a well-formed mind full of opinions and beliefs behind them. Last night had not been an anomaly. Whatever portion of him that hoped he'd merely been dazzled by the magic of a ballroom last night had been disappointed this afternoon.

Even in the bright light of day, Lilya exuded an extraordinary beauty. The delicate line of her jaw mixed with the fire of her eyes and the sensual set of her mouth to create a combination that was both utterly feminine and yet bespoke strength. For all her looks, one should not overlook the subtle power of her, a very attractive power none the less. It had taken a large part of his self-control to keep his attentions focused on Lady Eleanor today when he'd have liked nothing better than to follow the conversation between Lilya and Mr Agyros.

Perhaps he'd merely been too distracted by Mr Agyros's attentions towards Lilya. The man's eyes had nearly undressed Lilya with their perusal, his stare bordering on scandalous.

Beldon knew all too well from personal experience the kinds of thoughts Lilya's person could awaken in a man. Last night he'd not been immune to her charms. He was a man and he knew how men thought. Years ago, he'd spent the better part of a Season making sure Philippa didn't run afoul of ballroom bounders. He was more than well armed for the role of protector. But Lilya did not seem to need a protector. She had dealt aptly with Agyros's questions and with his own probe afterwards, making it very clear she was more capable than the usual débutante.

The last provided some level of intrigue. She'd thwarted Agyros's questions and that raised a question of its own—why would she want to avoid answering in the first place? What was she hiding? If she did have something to hide, it went some distance in explaining that attitude of worldliness he'd noted last night, that indefinable something, that subtle aura of power that set her apart from the other girls.

People who kept secrets for a long time had to be successful at deflection.

He was making enormous assumptions. For a man who prided himself on his logic, these speculations were beyond the pale of reason. First, he had no significant grounds on which to found his suppositions. He knew very little about Lilya's life before she'd come to live with Valerian. He might do well to keep it that way, too.

His behaviour last night had been totally unlike him. The consequence was obvious. He was distracted and tempted away from his plan, his whole purpose for coming to town. This would not do, but it was no less than he deserved for straying from the course. This is what one got for giving in to temptations. An antidote was in order. He must find a way to secure his wayward thoughts in her presence. Failing that, he must avoid her altogether until the details of his marriage were settled.

Chapter Three

Avoidance was proving impossible. Lilya Stefanov was a woman who *needed* watching. It was the only reasonable explanation for why Beldon found his gaze drifted towards the Latimore dance floor repeatedly where she spun in the arms of Christoph Agyros. There were other less reasonable explanations as well, but Beldon quickly discarded them. As a rule, he did not deal in the unreasonable.

He'd become the *de facto* chaperon tonight. Philippa had pled yet another headache and Val had taken her home earlier. Beldon wondered about the legitimacy of those 'headaches' just as he wondered if he'd have watched Lilya anyway.

He was developing an uncanny ability of knowing when Lilya was in a room and when she had left a room; a good ability for a chaperon to have especially when one's responsibility looked like Lilya. Positively entrancing in rose silk, she had drawn the gaze of more than one man in the ballroom tonight, Mr Agyros notably among them. The man practically had his eyes glued to her bosom, another reason why Beldon had his attentions riveted on them. It was a chaperon's job to cull the wheat from the chaff when it came to inappropriate attentions. If Mr Agyros didn't avert his gaze, he would soon find himself 'culled'. Agyros looked like the proverbial hungry man at a feast.

Agyros and Lilya whirled by the ballroom entrance and Beldon noticed the Braithmores enter as they passed. Lady Eleanor and her mother saw him and began the slow move his direction. Beldon tried to imagine that Lady Eleanor was already his wife. What would it be like to spot her across a room and know she was his? Certainly looking at her now did not conjure up a host of husbandly feelings. Would he develop an awareness of her presence, knowing when she left a room without actually seeing her go?

Their affections would grow over time as their companionship deepened. In theory that was how it was supposed to work. To date, the reality had been somewhat disappointing with Lady Eleanor. After all, what was the purpose of drives in the park and rounds of balls if not to get to know one another?

He'd had several opportunities to meet with her and he still felt he knew nothing about her.

Lady Eleanor and her mother approached as the set ended. Lady Eleanor would want to dance and he ought to oblige. Tonight, Lady Eleanor was dressed prettily in a gown of pastel pink with thin white ribbons for trim. She looked like a strawberry ice from Gunter's, smooth and unruffled. She always looked smooth and unruffled.

'Good evening, Lady Eleanor. You look delicious enough to eat.' Beldon bowed graciously over her hand. A man should be more than satisfied with such a lovely woman to call his wife. 'I believe the next dance is a waltz. Would you do me the honour?'

'It would be my pleasure.' Lady Eleanor blushed, looking so very young to his eye and yet there couldn't be more than a year or two between her and Lilya.

Lady Eleanor leaned forwards a little and said in a small whisper, 'Almack's granted me permission last week. May I confess? You'll be my first waltz at a real ball.'

'I am doubly honoured.' Beldon offered her his arm and escorted her on to the floor. He most properly placed his hand at her waist and felt her delicate touch at his shoulder, her flush deepening at the supposed intimacy of the contact.

'Do not worry over a thing, Lady Eleanor, I will

make sure your first waltz is most memorable,' he reassured her.

Lady Eleanor danced with perfunctory correctness. There was nothing wrong with her steps; still, Beldon couldn't help but compare her textbook movements with Lilya's fluid grace, his waltz with Lilya suddenly and vividly clear in his mind. There were other comparisons, too, that rose unbidden. He rather wished they hadn't.

Both women were as equally unknown to him, but there'd been nothing mechanical about his conversation with Lilya. She had looked him in the eye instead of over his shoulder. Their conversation topic had been nothing out of the ordinary and yet their conversation had flowed easily. There had been wit and laughter and something else indefinable he wasn't willing to name. He was using that word 'indefinable' quite a bit lately when it came to Lilya. For a man who liked a very defined world, it was an uncomfortable adjective.

'I think the decorations tonight are divine,' Lady Eleanor was saying. 'Pink roses are some of my favourite flowers.'

'Yes, pink looks especially nice on you.' Beldon turned his attentions back to Eleanor, back to the plan. He simply must try harder. It was not to his credit that he'd thought of little else except dancing with Lilya since last night. She'd felt exquisite in his arms, confident and sure of her physicality.

But it had been more than that. They'd *laughed* together. He wanted that moment again, although he suspected once more would not be enough. Such a need was not well done of him on the eve of proposing to another.

The waltz lasted an eternity. Lady Eleanor talked of decorations and gowns, her father's new carriage and her mama's new hat. Somewhere in the ballroom he heard Lilya laugh, a sound throaty and mellow like an aged whisky. His eyes roamed until he spotted her rose silk, her dark head tilted, contemplating something Mr Agyros had apparently leaned forwards and said, probably while the bounder stole another glance at her bosom.

He had every intention of extricating Lilya the moment the dance was over. He was the chaperon, after all. But when the dance ended, she was nowhere to be found. She and Mr Agyros had quietly disappeared from the ballroom.

There had been no way to refuse the request politely. The gardens would be well populated tonight with couples taking the air between heated dance sets. Christoph Agyros wasn't whisking her off to dark, unlit paths. In fact, anything remotely resembling seduction would be virtually impossible in the gardens. But there would be more privacy for conversation than what the crowded ballroom afforded. Lilya wanted to avoid that as much as she wanted to avoid the other. Too much refusal, though, would look odd.

'Fresh air would be delightful,' Lilya assented after they'd had taken a glass of punch on the sidelines. She'd caught sight of Beldon dancing beautifully with Lady Eleanor. There'd be no help from that quarter. She was on her own for the time being.

Outside, they walked along the paths, surrounded by others taking the night air. 'London and all its industry intrigue me.' Christoph waved his free arm in a generous sweep to encompass the garden. 'Does it captivate you as well?'

'I prefer the countryside and a quieter pace of life,' Lilya said, firmly shutting down that avenue of conversation.

He nodded in understanding. 'My family had a villa on Chios, before the troubles. I was fourteen, when...' he paused for effect and drew a deep breath before continuing '...when the trouble came. We lost the villa and much more in the reprisals, of course.'

Lilya could not help but be touched by his disclosure. All Phanariots knew what had happened at Chios, how the Ottomans had struck Chios in deliberate retaliation for the rebellion in Negush, the rebellion her father and others had led. Families had been killed, children orphaned, countless wealth lost. It had brought the Phanar to its knees.

'I'm sorry,' she said with quiet sincerity. Regardless of her inherent scepticism, she knew what it meant to lose family. She should not have doubted him. She had lost her family at Negush as he had lost his at Chios. She would never forget clutching baby Constantine to her and watching in frozen horror as her aunt and Alexei were cut down. She'd feared the same would happen to her but Valerian had been a veritable berserker, defending Dimitri Stefanov's children in that little copse of trees.

Christoph placed his hand over hers, the warmth of a private smile playing across his lips, his voice low and confidential. 'Thank you. Only those who have experienced such devastation firsthand can truly appreciate what those days meant to us and how we've had to rebuild a new life. We've been cast to all corners of Europe these days, and still we survive, yes?'

Survival was at stake right that moment, Lilya thought, staring up at Christoph Agyros's darkly handsome face. She worried that she'd made a tactical mistake. She had not told him where she was from when they'd met in the park. Yet he'd pushed ahead with his assumptions as if they'd been confirmed and she had not corrected him. Perhaps she should have. But a correction would have been a denial, a lie. If he discovered the truth later, he would wonder why she'd attempted the subterfuge. If he wasn't suspicious of her now, he would be then. If he was truly a diplomatic aide with no ties to the diamond, then she had nothing to fear from the admission. If he had darker purposes, he knew who she was already. A lie would be useless at best, a confirmation at worst. Only people with something to hide lied.

'My family was killed in Negush,' she admitted quietly, her decision made. They'd somehow managed to find a place slightly off the path. They were alone in the brightly lit garden.

'You are hesitant to talk of the past,' he said softly. 'Do not be ashamed. We have thrived. Like a phoenix, we have risen from the ashes.' His voice carried a quiet intimacy, his words attempting to bind them together. She could allow herself to take comfort in the moment, but she could not take more, could not trust him more. Not yet.

'Lilya,' he whispered her name, his hand gently cupping her cheek, his intentions unmistakable. He was going to kiss her. They both knew it. He was a handsome man and so far she had no reason to feel threatened. There was no motivation for her alarm, but it was there all the same.

A voice intruded, terse and sharp. 'Miss Stefanov, there you are.'

Beldon.

Lilya breathed a relieved sigh and stepped back out of reach at the sound of the familiar voice.

'We've got a dance coming up.' Beldon's tone brooked no disagreement. His eyes were cold as he took in Christoph Agyros. How much had Beldon seen? For no particular reason, it didn't sit well with her that he might have spied them on the brink of a kiss, unwanted as the kiss might have been.

Beldon held out his arm for her, offering her a reason to cross the pathway to join him. 'Give me a moment with Mr Agyros, please. There are a few things I need to explain to him.' His eyes were hard, looking past her to Christoph. Lilya complied, sensing argument would only serve to make her look foolish and to encourage Christoph. If she protested, Christoph would think she'd welcomed the kiss. With what she hoped looked like dignity, Lilya walked a discreet distance up the path and left Beldon to his 'business'.

Beldon's explanations did not take long and he soon materialised by her side. 'What, precisely, did you explain to Mr Agyros?' Lilya enquired, trying to sound affronted. The idea of Beldon meddling in her affairs left her feeling foolish in his presence. No doubt he considered her lacking in all sense to be caught almost-kissing an almost-stranger, especially when he knew she'd been wary of Mr Agyros in the park. He would wonder what kind of woman kissed a man she didn't trust or necessarily know.

'I explained to him that in our part of the world, a gentleman does not steal kisses on such short acquaintance and that a woman's reputation is taken most seriously.'

She heard the message hidden there for her. Real gentlemen protected a woman's reputation for her, but a woman had to guard her reputation as well. Lilya flushed at the subtle scolding.

Beldon's demeanour relaxed slightly. 'It's only that Val left me in charge. I would see you treated with the respect you deserve.' He paused, leaning his head close to her ear, his breath against her ear lobe sending a skittering sensation to her stomach. 'And I could see that you did not wish for things to progress further.'

She heard forgiveness in his words. He had not missed any of the nuances. He'd understood perfectly what had happened in the garden.

'No one kisses a woman against her will under my protection.'

There was a surprising ferocity in the hard set of his features that mirrored the power of his words. He was studying her with a male intensity that went beyond the scrutiny of a chaperon. For a moment, she envisioned she saw desire in his eyes, a desire for her that went beyond protection. Then it was gone. Of course, she must have been mistaken. He meant to pursue another. She'd seen him dancing with Lady Eleanor, all manners, nothing at all like the feral male who strode beside her now, his vaunted self-control threatening to slip its leash. All for her.

'Exactly what dance are we dancing?' Lilya attempted levity, hoping to restore her senses. She and Beldon were not themselves tonight. Beldon was a caged tiger, bristling with barely leashed fury. And she was no better, shivering at the sound of his voice near her ear, imagining hot desire in his eyes and, worse yet, welcoming it, wondering over it like the gaggles of women in the ballrooms who followed him everywhere with their eyes.

'A polka, I believe.' Beldon placed a hand at the small of her back to usher her through the door, his urbane manners reappearing the moment he set foot on the dance floor with her, the leash firmly back on his emotions. She envied him the ease with which he segued into politeness. No one would guess minutes ago he'd been out in the garden defending her jeopardised honour.

Lilya was glad the dance was a whirling polka, demanding all her energy. There wasn't time to talk, only to dance, and yet even then she was conscious of Beldon's every move: the flex of his shoulders, the muscles of his legs as they progressed through the steps. Perhaps it was a consequence of the Season and everyone being excessively marriage-minded that one couldn't help but consider every male as a possible mate, even ones that were off limits. For her, that meant all of them, but especially Beldon. This was the worst possible time to be distracted; Greece was poised on the brink of independence and a Phanariot stranger had sought out her attentions. It was definitely time to strap on a dagger.

Chapter Four

Christoph Agyros let himself out by way of the back gate. He would not be missed and he had much to think about. The *Filiki Adamao*, the Brotherhood of the Diamond, would be pleased to know he'd completed the first part of his mission: to locate the daughter of Dimitri Stefanov. The Stefanovs were one of the names that came up repeatedly throughout history where the diamond was concerned. He'd been dispatched to hunt her down once she'd disappeared. There were other names, too. It was not a guarantee the Stefanovs were the keepers of the diamond. Others had been sent to explore those avenues. Now it was up to luck.

The next step was to determine if she had the diamond. Christoph hoped so. He did not like to think he'd journeyed this far only to meet a red herring.

If it was his quarry that possessed the diamond, the possibilities were endless. He whistled in the darkness, trying to keep his thoughts from getting too far ahead.

The *Filiki Adamao* wanted the diamond for political reasons. They wanted the financial leverage to influence the next ruler, to set themselves up as the power behind the throne. They were a sentimental lot of older men. Sentiment and patriotism had its place, of course. But Christoph Agyros had a better cause: himself.

The idea had come to him during one of the many cold nights he'd spent on the road in inferior inns. He could claim the diamond for himself. After all, what had those old men done to retrieve the diamond? They'd plotted and planned, but in the end he'd endured the hardships. He'd been the one to attach himself to the Macedonian attaché once he'd arrived in London, a stroke of genius in hindsight. It had allowed him entrée into Lilya Stefanov's world— her very wealthy, privileged world.

The pretty Phanariot had done well for herself. Once the usual hiding places had been exhausted, the *Filiki Adamao* had suspected she'd run to England and her father's old friend. It was a long way to run, especially for a young woman alone. There had been some hope she'd be waylaid on the road, but she'd managed to reach England intact.

It didn't matter how far she ran. He'd find her.

Now that he'd seen her, a new plan was forming; if she had the diamond, he'd marry her. She might not even know he was after the diamond. She might believe he loved her. Women liked to believe in that twaddle and he was good at convincing them he did, too. It would, unfortunately, be a short marriage. The phrase 'until death to us part' was quite ambiguous about the length of the marital partnership. But at least it would be consummated. He would pay special attention to that detail.

The next step would be to court her with every ounce of his charm. He would make it a whirlwind romance, one that could justify a hasty marriage and quick departure back to the homeland in August, while attempting to ascertain her possession of the diamond. All this would be easier without her fierce protector. Lord Pendennys had made his position quite clear tonight. Christoph kicked at a loose pebble. It wasn't the first time Pendennys had shown an interest in Miss Stefanov. Christoph had been aware of Pendennys watching them that first day in the park.

Christoph shrugged in the darkness. If she didn't have the diamond, Pendennys could have her. But if she did, nothing would stand in his way, not even the good baron.

Beldon gave his cravat a final tug for good measure and shrugged into the carefully pressed morning coat of chocolate-brown superfine. It was time to step up his London campaign, as he was starting to refer to his plans for the Season. To do so, he needed to go shopping.

Beldon turned to his valet and took the driving gloves he offered. 'Thank you, Fredericks. I can handle everything from here.' He took the stairs with a rapid step, something shopping had never engendered in him before. But today was different. He was going to pick out a sincerity piece for Eleanor Braithmore and by doing so, firmly put errant thoughts of Lilya out of his mind. Goodness knew there were a million of them.

When he wasn't thinking of dancing with her, he was thinking of finding her in Christoph Agyros's arms, willowy and elegant, every man's most kissable fantasy with her head tilted up just so, her lips slightly parted. That particular sight had filled him with unmitigated fury. She had not looked fully committed to the idea of that kiss when he'd come upon them. Even if she had, he would have felt compelled to stop it. He was the chaperon, after all. He had his duties.

At least that's what he told himself.

In his more honest moments, he had his doubts.

Truth was, he'd wanted to be the man doing the kissing. The idea shocked him. He was not prepared for the magnitude of the revelation. *He wanted to kiss Lilya*. Wanted to do more than kiss her. Since the night he'd seen her delectable back, lust had been steadily growing, riding him hard in ways he was not used to. His reaction to Lilya was indeed stunning and unexpected, but it would resolve itself in time. She was merely a novelty to him. Eventually, the edge she raised in him would dull and fade.

Outside Pendennys House, his phaeton was waiting and Beldon swung confidently up on to the high seat in optimistic spirits. The best way to deal with temptations was to remove them altogether, hence the shopping trip. Thank goodness the sun was out.

He much preferred shopping in good weather if he had to shop at all. Squelching around in the mud and dashing between shop fronts dampened an experience he already found unenjoyable. Beldon pulled up in front of the Burlington Arcade with its uniformed guards and tossed the reins to his tiger. The Pendennys family jewellers, Messrs Bentham and Brown, were not far.

A doorman held open the door to the elite jewellers'. Ah, it was quiet in here, and private, a marked contrast from the busy street. Mr Brown came forwards to greet him personally when he stepped inside the shop.

Beldon had just taken a seat on a cushioned bench in front of the gem cases and explained his purpose when the door opened again. It was a small shop and Beldon could not help but turn to see the newcomer.

He stifled a groan of disbelief. Of all the jewellery shops in London, *she* had to walk into this one. In hindsight the odds were pretty good. It *was* the one Val and Philippa frequented. But who would have guessed she'd need a jeweller the same day he did? Fate had definitely made him her latest whipping boy. For all his efforts to drive Lilya from his mind, she seemed determined to keep showing up.

Lilya stepped forwards with a friendly smile, clearly feeling none of his angst over the encounter. 'Oh, hello, Beldon, fancy meeting you here.'

Chapter Five

When had she started calling him by his first name? Never mind that it sounded right. Beldon rose to his feet, playing the gentleman. 'Miss Stefanov, how good to see you. Are you enjoying the fine weather?' Good Lord, could he sound any more ridiculous? His greeting seemed extraordinarily stiff compared to her more effusive, warmer one.

She smiled again, but it didn't quite reach her eyes, a reminder that she was not the usual débutante; she was far more worldly, able to understand the underlying nuances of conversation. He had not called her Lilya and she took it as a subtle rebuke. 'The weather is lovely. We've had so little sun this year, it seems a special treat.'

The weather was duly dispatched and they stood facing one another for an awkward moment until Mr

Brown broke in. 'I'll get the viscount's things. My lord, I've laid out some trays if you'd like to begin looking.'

'Yes, thank you, Mr Brown.' Beldon turned back to the trays, immediately aware of his new dilemma. A gentleman did not ignore the presence of a lady, particularly when they were the only two people present. But a gentleman also did not discuss his affairs with a lady.

Lilya materialised at his side, having crossed the small space quietly. 'It is awkward, is it not? All this formality when we're not exactly strangers. It seems silly to have to pretend.'

It was on the tip of his tongue to ask precisely what they were when Mr Brown returned with a small package. 'Here are the rings the viscount had sent in to be reset.'

Lilya took the package. 'And the parure? Lady St Just said there would be two packages.'

Mr Brown excused himself again.

'Val and Philippa are having the St Just jewels remounted in more modern settings,' she explained. It was the perfect invitation to share his reason for being here. He chose to pass up the opportunity, but Lilya proved tenacious and perceptive.

'Are you selecting a betrothal piece?'

He felt compelled to correct her. 'No, there are jewels in the family vault for that. I merely wanted to select a sincerity piece.'

'That's a very kind gesture. I am sure whatever you choose will be lovely.'

That decreed a certain challenge. Would she tell him the truth if he picked something unacceptable? He had a rather perverse urge to find out. He picked up a necklace. 'I was thinking of this.'

The piece was pretty enough, but he knew it was wrong, too showy for his purposes. Would Lilya know? Would she say anything? A typical lady would not dare to contradict him. Lilya did not hesitate. She smiled and shook her head.

'Perhaps *after* you're officially engaged,' she said gently. 'A necklace is too sophisticated, I think, for your intentions at present.'

Something dangerous and volatile sparked to life between them. He should leave well enough alone, but the devil in him was already awake and wanting his due. How would she handle it?

'What are those intentions?' Beldon asked in gravelly tones more appropriate for seduction than shopping. Truly he knew better than to stoke this ambiguous fire she roused in him.

'You tell me. They're *your* intentions.' She studied him with sharp eyes, missing nothing of the innuendo, of the change in the atmosphere between them.

There it was. She'd called him out. This was his chance to declare himself. What a bold piece she was and yet she pulled off that boldness without seeming unladylike. Really, it was quite admirable.

Mr Brown returned with the second package. He handed it to Lilya and noted the necklace still dangling from Beldon's hand. 'Ah, you've made a choice, then? The necklace is very nice.'

Beldon skewered the smaller man with an imperial stare, his voice cold. 'Very nice, but very wrong for my cause,' he corrected. 'A decent gentleman would not give such a piece to his bride.'

The man had the good grace to colour at the implication: he'd been caught toadying.

'Perhaps something in pink?' Lilya offered. It was meant to be a helpful suggestion, but Beldon saw the challenge behind it. Pink could only be for one person. But Lilya was right and Beldon saw no reason to disagree. A pink gem would be lovely and meaningful to Lady Eleanor. As long as they didn't say Lady Eleanor's name out loud, it wasn't as if he was outright asking one woman to help him select jewellery for another.

Trays were taken away and others brought out from behind the locked cabinet, far more than he'd expected. He'd not anticipated such a variety. In tacit agreement, he and Lilya sat back down on the bench.

'A ring, then?' Beldon randomly chose one of the dozens of rings on display, suddenly less interested in what had brought him here in the first place and more interested in Lilya's response. He had jewels aplenty in the Pendennys vault. He would save those for a wedding gift, or an anniversary gift. The Pendennys emeralds were heavy pieces. Every time he thought of Lady Eleanor in them, he imagined her bent over from the weight of them. They were not jewels for a girl.

Lilya laughed sweetly and took pity on him. 'A bracelet or a pin would be best.' She motioned to the jeweller. 'You can put away all the trays but these three here.'

'I can see that I would have made a disaster of this on my own.' He should not have said that. It was entirely wrong, entirely too familiar. He was joking with her as if they were friends when everyone knew a man could *not* be friends with a lady. He could feel his jaw tightening. It was too easy to be charmed by Lilya—by her graceful gestures, by the subtle way she'd taken control of the situation.

She threw him a sidelong glance as if to say she doubted that, that she was on to his game of provoking her. Her eyes danced with an implicit understanding of their secret game. She turned back to study the trays. 'This coral-and-pearl piece would be perfect.'

It was indeed quite the perfect piece: a cameo habille, a jewel within a jewel. Beldon could find no quarrel with it. He would have selected it himself, left to his own devices. In spite of the game he played with Lilya, he did know a thing or two about jewellery. The cameo was of angelskin coral in the palest shades of pink, a tiny stone of pink jasper set on the cameo's bosom giving it the jewel within a jewel. Eleanor would be able to wear it pinned to a gown.

Lilya leaned forwards and spoke quietly, a finger tracing the fine lines of the cameo. 'What better way to tell her of your feelings than that you view her as your very own jewel within a jewel, a woman you love as much for her beauty on the outside as her beauty on the inside?'

The sentiment surprised him. Is that what women saw in jewellery? No wonder they coveted it. Did men have any idea what secret messages they were sending? More importantly, is that what *he* meant by giving Lady Eleanor this gift? Admittedly, Lilya's words had something of a shocking effect on him. The sentiment she expressed was noble and fine. But could he give Lady Eleanor such a gift, knowing the message behind it to be a lie? He hoped such sentiment would be true eventually. As of today, it was not. He had no idea if Lady Eleanor was a lovely person on the inside. She was precisely what she'd been bred to be, a blank slate for her husband to write on. A blanker slate, Beldon could not imagine. He simply didn't know. He knew only that she fit his criteria. He stilled for a moment, a horrible thought coming to him.

What if your criteria are wrong? What if you need more? The thought was practically blasphemous. He should not even give credence to it. But there'd been a lot already today he should not have done, starting with allowing Lilya to sit down beside him. He'd played with fire and now he was getting burned, absolutely and thoroughly scorched.

'What is it? You look pale all of a sudden.' Lilya unconsciously placed a hand on his arm, her face full of concern within the frame of her bonnet. 'I hope you're not coming down with a spring cold. Philippa won't forgive you if you get sick before Val's Rose Gala. She's spent days planning it to celebrate his new hybrid.'

Stubbornly, Beldon pushed the traitorous idea aside. There was no room for doubt. He stood up, shaking off Lilya's hand. 'I'm quite fine. The cameo is perfect. Mr Brown, I would like to have it wrapped up so I may take it right away.'

He must forgo the pleasure of such doubts. This moment of weakness was nonsense. More than one man had been the recipient of cold feet. It was part and parcel of the engagement ritual and the embracing of the unknown. He told himself it was actually nice to get cold feet. It reminded him of how important this decision was. It was worthy of being agonised over. If it was something that could be hastily done, everyone would do it.

The jeweller returned with the cameo in a small blue velvet box tied prettily with a pale blue ribbon. 'I've done it up neatly for you, my lord. The ladies put as much store in the wrapping as they do what's actually inside the box.' He chuckled.

Beldon tucked the box into his coat pocket. The package was small enough not to draw attention. No one would even know he had it with him. He could carry it with him discreetly and wait for the right moment. Or, came the errant thought, he could forget about it, letting it lie unclaimed in a pocket for, oh, say ages, and no one would be the wiser.

'Ahem, my lord, if I may be so bold, I happened to notice this piece in the back. We haven't displayed it yet. I just acquired it a few days ago from a gem dealer. Since you were looking for something pink, I wanted to show it to you—it's a bracelet of silver and tourmaline.'

Lilya gasped, enchanted at the sight of it. 'It's beautiful.'

Encouraged, the jeweller went on, 'It is straight from Burma and the mines of Mynnamar. If I might, Miss Stefanov?' The jeweller deftly draped the bracelet about her wrist, but struggled with the clasp.

'Here, allow me,' Beldon volunteered unthinkingly. He reached out, gently capturing her wrist, and fastened the bracelet, but not without marveling at the feel of her fine, narrow bones beneath her glove. Her wrist was as delicate and slender as the bracelet itself—a perfect match that sent a jolt of unmistakable desire straight to his male core. Beldon stepped back, hoping to distance himself.

Lilya held up her wrist, the deep shades of the

tourmaline catching the light. The bracelet slid towards her elbow. 'It's a little big.'

'Links can be removed easily if it's too large,' Mr Brown put in quickly, no doubt smelling another sale in the air, or perhaps something else Beldon did not care to give name to. Beldon did not care for the suggestion Mr Brown intimated, that somehow he'd be purchasing jewellery also for Lilya. The assumption carried with it an inappropriate implication about the nature of their relationship.

'It's a beautiful piece, sir, thank you for sharing it. But I will pass. The bracelet is not in my intended's style.' Beldon was careful to emphasise the 'my intended' part. It wasn't a lie. The bracelet was entirely wrong. It was too elegant, too subtle, too rich in colour, for an English rose like Lady Eleanor. The piece needed someone with dark hair and slightly foreign looks to be carried off. The piece needed someone like Lilya. Beldon could not imagine the bracelet on another's wrist after seeing it on hers and that was dangerous ground indeed. It was time to go.

'I am ready for sustenance, how about you?' Beldon said, betraying none of the comparisons dominating his mind at the moment. He helped Lilya with the bracelet clasp and returned it to the jeweller. 'May I interest you in a stop at Fortnum and Mason's before we head home?'

* * *

Ah, he'd chosen wisely, Beldon thought twenty minutes later. Tea was precisely the thing he needed to restore his balance. He could not recall the last time he'd enjoyed sitting down to flavoured hot water and little sandwiches so much. If he'd been alone, he would have taken refreshment at his club over on St James's. The meal would have been more substantial, but the company less so.

'You knew more about jewels than I realised. Your taste was impeccable,' Beldon complimented as they finished their second pot. It was nearly time to go. He could not justify lingering any longer.

Lilya blushed becomingly, but her eyes darkened and Beldon sensed she was holding an internal debate with herself. Fine. He would wait. At last, aware that he wasn't going to fill the silence until she spoke, she said, 'My family dealt in jewels in Negush and, before that, my grandfather was a jeweller to the sultan in Constantinople.'

The admission stunned him into silence. She said it as naturally as if she'd said, 'My family own dairy cows in Herefordshire'.

'I never knew' was all he could manage. Maybe he'd have to call for a third pot of tea after all. One didn't just get up from the table and leave a comment like that unexplored.

'You don't talk of your life very much and yet I think your life has been full of fascinating experiences. Certainly, very different experiences than what one has here.' Beldon held her eyes across the table, wanting her to see the sincerity in his own, wanting to see the veils lift from hers. The more he knew her, the more mysterious she became. There were depths here. 'I would like to hear about them. You don't have to forget about them simply because you're in England now.'

'It is all in the past and sometimes forgetting can be better than remembering.'

But surely not better than never knowing. Beldon would not be put off. 'Jewels are not a poor man's trade. What was your father to the empire?' He gave in to the inevitable and signalled for another pot of tea.

Then, just as she had in the jewellery store when he'd deliberately selected the wrong piece, Lilya smiled and took pity on him. In soft tones of confidentiality she said, 'We were *hospodars*. Do you know the word?' Beldon shook his head. Her next words took his breath away altogether. 'We were princes.'

The disclosure all but flattened him. She'd been born to great wealth and privilege and then it had all been taken away. This was not what he'd expected. He'd envisioned her raised in modest surroundings, middle class, perhaps, with a merchant father caught up in the intrigues of larger men. He'd attributed her nervousness to feeling overwhelmed by the jewels, out of her element, but clearly that was not the case. Her taste had been far too exquisite and this recent revelation confirmed it.

She was used to riches.

Lilya continued and Beldon listened intently for fear that she'd stop and he'd not get another chance to hear her answer. 'We had our trade, but we also were responsible for collecting taxes for the sultan in our region.' She shrugged here. 'Many of the ruling families abused their power in being tax collectors. But the Stefanovs were always fair.'

She was used to power.

Riches and power. A deadly combination. And one that might explain the glimpse of worldliness he sometimes saw in her eyes, the way she carried herself with a certain degree of pride and confidence not found in the usual débutante.

She was not willing to say more and adroitly turned the conversation to his estate, plying him with questions regarding the upgrades and new technologies he was employing for higher crop yields.

'I can see you love your home,' Lilya said after a while. 'I think it's good for a lord to care so much for his people. A good leader is always ready to put his needs aside for the benefit of the people.' She poured out the last of the tea, only getting half a cup. 'Oh dear, I think we've drunk half the tea in England.'

Beldon laughed, the austere line of his mouth turning up into an approachable grin.

'You should do that more often,' Lilya remarked.

'Do what?'

'Laugh. Smile.'

'I laugh. I smile,' Beldon protested.

'Not nearly enough. You have a wonderful smile, it was one of the things I noticed about you when we danced at the Fitzsimmons' ball.'

'And Mr Agyros? Does he have a wonderful smile as well?' He was stoking the fires again. Lilya looked as if she'd been struck. It was not well done of him. He wished immediately he could take the words back.

Lilya stood up and gathered her things. Her tone was frigidly formal. 'If I was not clear then, let me be clear with my gratitude now. I appreciated your interference although it was not necessary.'

Beldon rose along with his temper. He was angry with himself and this current gambit of theirs made an easy target. 'My *interference*? Is that what you call it?'

'What would you prefer I call it?' Lilya said, undaunted.

'How about "intervention"? "Interference" implies I was sticking my nose where it wasn't wanted.'

'Perhaps you were.'

'Would you have preferred letting Mr Agyros kiss you?'

'I can handle myself with a gentleman. Nothing would have proceeded without my permission.' Lilya gave her hair a regal toss. 'Now, I think it best you take me home. I want to make sure Philippa is feeling better. She was feeling poorly when I left this morning.'

He promptly left Lilya after a short visit with his sister to assure himself of her health. But his day seemed decidedly empty after that. Beldon had no appetite for the social engagements on his calendar that evening and he opted for a night in, poring over atlases in his library and searching his shelves for books about the Ottoman Empire and the *hospodars*.

That night he dreamed of a dark-haired woman wearing only the Pendennys emeralds.

In the morning, he sent a hurried note to Mr Brown. He'd take the tourmaline bracelet after all.

Chapter Six

By the evening of Val's Rose Gala, Lilya was
starting to doubt her ability to avoid an engagement
without causing a nasty scandal. A few weeks into
the Season and she was worried about lasting until
August. When she'd laid her plans, she had under-
estimated the issue of time. Three months, twelve
weeks at the most, had not seemed such a great
amount then. She had not realised just how different time was in the *ton*. Two weeks was a lifetime,
three an eternity. The breath of scandal tumbled
débutantes from their pedestals at dizzying speeds
and courtships were alarmingly accelerated. Life
was lived fast during the Season and decisions made
even faster.

Lilya stood in Val's drawing room, surrounded
by her court of guests and all too aware of the subtle

change in her circumstances. Two weeks ago, she'd been ably deflecting any marked interest of would-be suitors. Admittedly, some of those suitors had been lukewarm in their attentions, unsure of her suitability. She was not one of them, no matter what the size of Val's dowry. She understood that, it had worked to her benefit.

Men might flock to a lovely woman, might even admire her, but she knew in the end some things mattered more than others when a peer contemplated marriage. She'd counted on that. But somewhere in the past month she'd gone from 'potential' wifely material to 'acceptable' and it was all Beldon's fault, never mind that he'd made himself scarce since the day at the jewellers'. He'd danced with her on two different occasions. People had noticed and the damage was done.

Every match-making mama in London knew Lord Pendennys had come to town to take a wife, thus any girl he showed attentions towards must be a decent choice. It followed that any girl worthy of Pendennys's high standards was worthy of the attentions of others, too.

The consequence was that her court was now filled with genuine suitors who were definitely looking to take home a wife in August. Among them, Christoph Agyros, who'd not overstepped his bounds since the night at Latimore's.

Lilya took a modest sip of the pre-supper champagne Val was serving in honour of the occasion, letting her eyes scan the group around her. Christoph stood beside her in what he was starting to assume was his place of honour. Beldon was notably missing as he had been for the last week. He would be here tonight, she knew. He wouldn't miss Val's big party. The idea that Beldon would be here sent a shiver of anticipation through her. She wished she could like Christoph more. There was no reason not to. They had much in common and he was handsome with good prospects in the import-export business. If things were different, he'd be ideal.

Come now, be fair, her conscience chided. If things were different, she'd still be drawn to Beldon. Different wouldn't change that attraction, just make it more possible to act upon. In which case, she was better off without 'different'. An attraction to Beldon could easily lead to a broken heart if she gave her feelings their head.

She felt him before she saw him, some nebulous sixth sense telling her Beldon had entered the room and gone straight to Valerian. Her eyes surreptitiously followed him. How could they not? He was the finest man in the room. Impeccable in dark evening wear, his hair burnished and smooth in the light, he commanded attention with his very presence. He spoke with Val and then made his way towards her.

'Miss Stefanov, our host has asked me to take you into supper.'

Her court groaned their mutual disappointment, but could do nothing to forestall the inevitable loss. She took Beldon's arm and they prepared for the summons to dinner.

'Do you think you might call me Lilya any time soon?'

'Not in public company,' Beldon replied, his eyes forwards. 'By the way, you look lovely in green. That gown becomes you.'

'Not just green, *celery*,' Lilya corrected playfully.

'Ah, celery. Why not broccoli? If we're naming colours after vegetables, why stop with celery?'

'But we have.'

'Stopped?'

'No, named. We have named other colours from nature. There's peach, strawberry, lemon-yellow, grape.'

'*Those* are fruits,' Beldon interrupted with mock seriousness. 'I believe we were talking about vegetables.'

Lilya laughed. 'Well, there's aubergine.'

'Aubergine? Is that all you can come up with? This seems highly iniquitous to vegetables everywhere. Fruits have a clear monopoly on fashion.'

'Herbs, too,' Lilya put in, warming to the word-play. 'Lavender, sage-green, mustard-yellow, saffron.'

'Careful, saffron's technically a spice.'

'Careful,' she repeated, unable to refuse a final tease. 'You're on the brink of a smile.'

'I smile.'

'A reactionary defence.'

'What is? Smiling?'

'Your answer. You're just disagreeing to disagree. You never smile.'

'I do. I've smiled three times at least that you've commented on.'

'Maybe you only smile with me,' Lilya ventured in the spirit of playful sparring, but it had the opposite effect.

He reached over to cover her hand with his where it lay upon his sleeve, another of his proper but arousing gestures. 'Maybe I do. What do you suppose that means, Miss Stefanov?'

There was little of the gentleman in the low-voiced growl. They were doing it again, sparking the thrum of tension that could ignite so readily between them. But to what purpose? This was an exciting but futile game they played. It begged the question whether he played this game with all the females of his acquaintance. More importantly, did he play this game with Lady Eleanor?

'Have you given Lady Eleanor the pin yet?' she asked quietly.

'Not yet,' Beldon replied, the tight set of his jaw subtly indicating he was well aware of the underplay in their conversation. The butler announced dinner, putting a timely end to further discussion. But the answer was plenty of food for thought throughout dinner.

Not yet.

He'd had a week to find the right moment and yet he hadn't.

'Is there something on your mind?' Christoph enquired quietly. He'd been seated on her other side for dinner at the long table. No doubt Philippa had thought to do her a favour.

'I was just contemplating the fish but, alas, you've cod me at it.' She smiled, but Christoph merely looked confused. She suddenly felt silly. '"Cod", "caught"—the two words sound alike,' she explained hastily.

Beldon would have laughed.

Admittedly, it was not a hilarious joke, but it was worth a chuckle.

'I see.' Christoph forced a smile and Lilya felt that he did see, not the joke, but something more—that he'd been compared and come up lacking.

He was losing her. Christoph wasn't sure how it had happened. He'd felt they'd got off to a good start a few weeks ago. Since then, he'd danced attendance on her, sent flowers, done all the things a lady liked. And yet Lilya Stefanov hadn't opened up to him, given him no inkling of her ties to the diamond, which in itself was telling. Lilya shared nothing of her history with him, although he'd given her plenty of chances to do so. He knew no more about her than what was already in the *Filiki Adamao* dossier. Saying nothing at all did arouse his suspicions.

Christoph did lay the blame for his lack of headway at Baron Pendennys's proverbial doorstep. Christoph was man enough to feel the challenge in it. Beldon might fancy himself her protector, but that was not all. The Englishman lusted for her. Those feelings did not go unreciprocated. Whenever Pendennys was present, Lilya's attentions were riveted in his direction.

Her choice, to favour the baron over him, was undermining his original plans. He'd decided if she would not be forthcoming about the diamond, he would have to take a different measure and he would do it tonight. Tonight would be the perfect opportunity to search the St Just town house. If he could find the diamond, his worries would be over. He would simply steal it and he could forgo any semblance of relationship with Lilya. He would merely fade out of her life, called back to his country by some imaginary emergency. He might even be gone before she noticed the diamond was missing.

There were only a few places the diamond would be: St Just's office in a secret vault, assuming St Just knew about the gem's existence, or in Lilya's own rooms.

There was always the chance, too, that if St Just knew about the diamond, the diamond was not on the premises, but in a bank safe under security. That would be his next step.

The worst case was that the diamond had been left in Cornwall. No, Christoph corrected, worst case was not finding the diamond at all.

If that happened, he would have to ask Lilya outright and he'd need a believable relationship in place to do it without giving away his hand. Only a woman in love would not view such a question as suspicious. If Lilya's suspicions were aroused, it would be war, all illusions of courtship banished in the wake of reality, and his mission exposed to the world. He had as much to gain from secrecy as Lilya did, provided she actually possessed the diamond.

All things considered, Christoph was relieved when the dinner came to an end. The men would not linger over port and brandy tonight with the promise of the fireworks at the reception and the revealing of the new flower.

The viscount rose from his chair and clinked his spoon against a crystal glass. 'We'll forgo brandy tonight in light of our other entertainments. I am told guests are already assembling in the gardens for the unveiling.' He gave a little speech about the rose, one Christoph felt certain would be repeated later at the greenhouse, and then the company paraded out to the grounds.

Christoph made sure to attach himself to a large group so that Lilya would be less likely to notice his absence when he slipped away, although she was so distracted by the baron tonight, she might not notice at all.

As the group exited to the verandah, Christoph made his move and extricated himself, falling back until he was alone in the house. He'd start in the study on the second floor.

Christoph made straight for the moderately sized oil on the study wall. If there was a safe behind it, there would be a lock that needed picking. This was where he'd spend most of his time. Lock picking was the domain of the patient man. Christoph lifted down the painting and breathed a sigh of relief. There was a safe with a standard tumbler lock. Ah, the viscount had good taste. The lock appeared to be one of the quite fine specimens turned out by the French. He could pick it, but that would take some time, especially if it indeed was French. He might be better served to take a quick look around for a key. Sometimes the easiest road was precisely that—easy.

Out of caution, Christoph hung the picture back up. There was no sense in giving himself away until he was ready. Christoph sat behind Valerian's desk and began a cursory search of the drawers. People usually had a very predictable habit of keeping their keys close to the items the keys unlocked.

In the second drawer, he found what he was looking for in a small wooden box pushed to the back: a set of keys. That was where Christoph's luck ended. The safe held no sign of the diamond.

Christoph was missing. The man was absent from his post at Lilya's side. Beldon's eyes swept the crowd. True, there were nearly two hundred people gathered in the St Just gardens. He could be among the crowd anywhere. It wasn't mandated he had to stand with Lilya, but it seemed odd for him not to be.

It might be nothing more than a need to relieve himself. Still, with the lure of fireworks looming, Beldon thought it was taking the man a rather long time to take care of his business. Fireworks were a treat even for adults and St Just's promised to be well worth the wait.

Beldon discreetly headed back to the house. He enquired of the servants. No one had seen anyone return to the house. Beldon made a quick survey of the public rooms downstairs. They turned up no sign of Val's errant guest. But if he'd felt indisposed or come down with a headache, he'd be unlikely to lie down in those rooms. He would seek a darker room where he could be left alone. Even though logic supported the conclusion, Beldon didn't like the idea of Christoph in the private areas of the town house unescorted. The man wasn't family and it seemed somehow presumptuous.

Beldon headed upstairs. The library or Val's office seemed likely guesses. Both would be dark and complete with the requisite sofa for the occasional nap. But he doubted Val would like anyone poking around in his private affairs.

Val's office appeared empty, but on a whim Beldon took a minute to search for signs that someone had been there recently. Ah, most curious, he thought. The sofa showed no signs of a depression, but the chair behind Val's desk still held body heat and an oil landscape of horses and hounds on the wall was a fraction crooked. Someone had been here and not to rest.

Above him, a floorboard creaked. The bedrooms were directly over the office. Beldon's logic told him it could be maids readying the chambers for bed. But in light of the odd circumstances in Val's office, Beldon wasn't ready to dismiss the floorboard without investigation.

The first boom heralded the beginning of the fireworks display. If someone was snooping around, they'd picked a good time to do it. Beldon took the stairs to the upper floor two at a time. At the top of the stairs, Beldon slowed. He would need stealth up here. If Christoph was slinking around, it would not serve to announce his presence.

As it turned out, no stealth was needed. Halls were straight, open places with no inherent cover. Christoph was still out in the open, his back to Beldon as he went down the left side of the corridor. Beldon watched for a moment. Lilya's room was on that side and further down. It was time to announce his presence.

'The fireworks are *downstairs*,' Beldon called out.

Christoph halted, his body stiffening at the unexpected sound of a voice. Even in the dim light of the hall, Beldon could see he'd been taken at unawares. Perhaps he should have waited and followed Christoph to see what the bounder was up to. Whatever it was, it was no good. A gentleman didn't sneak upstairs to a young woman's bedchamber with honourable intentions in mind.

Christoph turned slowly. 'Ah, Pendennys, I'd got lost.' He put a hand to his head. 'I was looking for a place to lie down while the others enjoyed the entertainment.' He shrugged, letting the gesture finish his thought.

Christoph walked towards him, ostensibly returning to the stairs to rejoin the group outside, but Beldon's body tensed in awareness. Christoph didn't walk like a man pained by a headache. His step was firm, his shoulders straight. His hand reached into an inside jacket pocket.

Good God, did the man have a weapon on him? Beldon didn't fear for himself. He could hold his own in any fight, even one with unequal odds. His concern was for Lilya. Had Val unsuspectingly left her alone with an armed man on previous occasions? Had Christoph carried a weapon that night he'd taken Lilya into the garden? What kind of gentleman went armed to social functions?

'There's nothing up here but the private bedchambers.' Beldon's statement was more accusation than fact.

'You would know,' Christoph sneered. He was close enough now for Beldon to see his eyes, hard and alert. Definitely not the eyes of a man feeling unwell.

'What do you mean by that?' Beldon challenged. A fight was coming. The comment was meant to provoke and he was ready to be provoked. Beldon stepped in front of the stairs, arms crossed, legs spread in a defiant stance. Christoph wasn't getting down the steps until he had answers.

'I mean, you're besotted with her.' Christoph looked positively cruel now, his face suffused with anger. Anger at being thwarted in some plan or thwarted at love?

'Besotted? With Miss Stefanov? I think you misunderstand,' Beldon said carefully. He would not give Agyros the satisfaction.

'Do I? You know where her bedroom is, you dance with her. I see you watch her with your eyes whenever she's in a room, how you look for her when she's not.' Christoph paused here for effect. 'You could not bear to see her kiss another that night in the garden.'

'I am a family friend. I have her best interests at heart, which is more than I can say for you at the moment,' Beldon ground out, his own anger reaching a dangerous level. He would fight, but he would not throw the first punch in Valerian's home.

Christoph's eyes glinted dangerously. 'It's a convenient shield to hide your true feelings behind.'

'And your true intentions? What really brings you up here to lurk in private quarters?' Beldon was starting to rethink the whole philosophy of not throwing the first punch.

Christoph gave another of his irritating shrugs. His eyes shifted slightly to the ground for the briefest of moments. 'I was going to leave a small gift for her as a surprise.' He looked up accusingly at Beldon. 'I suppose that's ruined now. How pleased you must be with yourself.' Christoph shoved past Beldon, bumping him in the shoulder.

'You lie.' Beldon's hand came up, restraining Christoph and perhaps, oh, so subtly—or not—shoving him back so that they were now in the corridor, away from the mouth of the stairs. They could fight here without fear of falling down the stairs.

'That is an affront to my honour,' Christoph growled.

'Show me the gift.'

'This is none of your affair.' Christoph reached

for his inner pocket again. Beldon did not wait to see if it was a gift or a gun. If he waited, it would be too late. Beldon launched himself at Christoph, prohibiting the attempt to retrieve anything from a pocket. The men went down together on the carpet, rolling and grappling. Christoph was a smart fighter, showing off a prowess that spoke of far too many similar encounters, but Beldon had backed Valerian in several fights before and he proved the stronger. Beldon straddled the man, finally succeeding in pinning him to the floor. He flipped open Christoph's coat and reached inside. It was as he'd expected.

'A very strange gift, I'd say. Special custom of your country?' Beldon stepped back, feeling confident Christoph wouldn't try anything desperate while he held the gun. Beldon checked the gun. Loaded and primed. His dislike for Christoph rose another notch. The bastard had brought a primed weapon into Valerian's home.

Christoph scrambled to his feet. 'You know nothing about me or where I've come from. If you did, you might understand why a gentleman feels it necessary to go well armed even among a genteel public. I did not come to cause trouble.'

Beldon quirked an eyebrow in cold disdain. 'But clearly you thought it might find you anyway.'

Christoph moved past him and this time Beldon let him go. The fireworks were ending and the others would be returning indoors. His confrontation with Christoph was effectively ended for now.

Part way down the stairs, Christoph turned back. 'This is something Lilya understands. We are alike, she and I.'

Beldon waited until Christoph had rejoined the early returning guests before he headed downstairs. He needed a moment to collect himself. Christoph's comments rankled. Beldon despised the implication that Lilya was like Christoph in any sense. If he was generous, he'd give Christoph the benefit of the doubt. Perhaps the man might carry a gun out of a habitual need for self-protection. But that did not change the fact that Christoph was a liar. He'd lied about the gift and hence he'd lied about his reason for being upstairs, skulking towards Lilya's room.

What else had Christoph lied about? In his experience liars told more than one lie. The man must be investigated.

There was something else that must be investigated, too: his feelings for Lilya. Christoph had lied about much, but was there some truth in those claims? He had not realised how much he'd let it show. He had not intended that. Then again, Christoph might have been taking a random guess. Christoph had been baiting him on purpose. It was taking things too far to put any amount of stock in Christoph's angry suppositions. Now was not the time for speculation. Now was the time to go after Agyros.

Chapter Seven

The bastard managed to slip out seconds ahead of him under the protection of a group headed off to the Chester rout. He could add 'coward' to the growing list of adjectives describing the bounder. Beldon cursed his bad luck and withdrew to the drawing room to wait out the farewelling.

From his vantage point he could see Lilya standing with Val and Philippa talking to the last of the guests. She was leaning forwards to catch elderly Lady Cotsworth's words, giving the older woman all of her attention, the expression on her face genuine and sincere—trademarks of an excellent hostess. He had not thought of her in that light although in hindsight he should have. She'd spent the time since her arrival in England being mentored by Philippa, the consummate hostess. Was it possible he'd over-

looked ways in which Lilya fit one of his criteria?
There was some relief in that. It would mean his
earlier concerns over a flawed criterion were now
mitigated. The criteria was fine, it was merely the
application of it that erred.

But there was still the second hurdle. Her money.
His principles. Her money came from Val and he
could not in good conscience take money from his
best friend. He still needed it. He'd been counting
on a good marriage to bring the comfort of extra
funds to Pendennys. He'd done much to make Pendennys solid again, but there were limits to what
even he could manufacture. The mining investments
he relied on currently would not always pay out, a
truth his father had not recognised. He would not be
caught out by the same fault.

The clock in the hall had chimed half past eleven
by the time the door shut behind the last guest. The
evening had been delightful and early by *ton* standards, as a supper and reception should be. The butler
closed the door behind the last guest and Val let out
a sigh. 'Well, that's that.' He bent to kiss Philippa's
cheek. 'Well done, my love. It was a splendid evening.'

Philippa smiled at him, blue eyes laughing with a
secret clearly between the two of them. 'The evening
isn't over yet. Perhaps you should reserve judgement
until later.'

Beldon felt distinctly *de trop* at moments such as these, as if he were an intruder on a private scene. He 'ahemmed' in the drawing-room doorway. 'Before you two start mooning over each other, perhaps we might talk a while.' He silently regretted being the bearer of news that would delay whatever Val was anticipating upstairs.

'Shall I ring for tea?' Philippa asked once they were settled in the drawing room on a comfortable grouping of chairs near the fireplace.

'Only if you like.' Beldon made a dismissive wave with his hand. 'No need to on my account.'

'Perhaps something stronger, then?' Val didn't wait for an answer before sending a footman off for a decanter and glasses. Val turned his attention back to Beldon. 'Well, out with it. Clearly something is afoot,' Val said without preamble. 'I noticed you missed the fireworks.'

'There was an intruder here this evening.' Beldon looked each of them in the eye, but his gaze settled on Lilya and remained, wanting to see her reaction in full. 'I caught Christoph Agyros upstairs.'

'Caught?' Val queried. 'An interesting choice of words. Do you suppose you might just as well say "found" him up there? You must agree, "caught" carries a certain guilty connotation with it.'

Beldon's gaze flickered to Valerian briefly. 'Yes, "caught" is the word I mean. He was walking down the left side of the corridor, counting doors. He'd reached number three when I came upon him.'

Lilya stifled a gasp of surprise. Beldon's eyes were back on her, watching her for a reaction. There were only four rooms on that side of the hall. With only one room left, the implication was clear. Christoph had been looking for her room, and, even more telling, Christoph had known where to find it. Lilya hazarded a glance in Valerian's direction. He knew it, too. Years of work in diplomacy had enhanced Val's intuitive skill to read beyond the words to the message within the message.

The anxiety Lilya had kept under constant control since fleeing her homeland slipped its leash, running rampant in a moment of panic. Was Christoph her fears incarnate? Had she indeed been found? A thousand questions vied for her attentions.

'Did you question him?' Val asked Beldon.

Beldon nodded. The grim set of his jaw boded ill news. 'He said he wanted to surprise Lilya with a gift, a token of his affections.'

Beldon was watching her too closely. Lilya struggled to hide her growing fear. How would she explain all this to them? What explanation could she possibly offer that would not reveal the diamond and her true reasoning for coming to England? The pleasantness of the evening faded. The joy she'd taken in the fireworks, evaporated entirely. Surely that had been when Christoph had slipped away. She had not realised he was gone until she'd seen him back at the house with a group of people who'd gone inside earlier. While she'd been taking a moment's enjoyment, he'd been searching the house. More precisely, he'd been searching out her chambers, perhaps knowing what he would find there.

Be careful, she cautioned herself. She must not jump to conclusions quite yet.

'Do we know what that gift was?' Val's tone was cool and alert. He and Beldon looked ready to pummel someone on her behalf. This was exactly what Lilya wanted to avoid.

'There was no gift.' Beldon reached into his jacket, giving Philippa an apologetic look. 'I did not believe him and we brawled.'

Philippa gave a chagrined gasp. 'At my party?'

'It was a small tussle. Nothing was broken,' Beldon said ruefully in a way that made Lilya think he wasn't talking about vases, but perhaps noses. 'There was no gift in his pocket, only this.'

Lilya jumped in spite of herself at the sight of the gun. There was regret in Beldon's eyes, but his tone did not soften. 'I am sorry for my briskness, Lilya. I would not frighten you for the world. If it's any consolation, I don't think Christoph meant to use the gun proactively. I certainly don't think he came here with the intention to shoot you.'

'Did he offer an explanation?' Philippa broke in. 'A gun at a reception is most unorthodox.'

'He said it was commonplace in his world. I did not fully believe him. But I kept the gun.' Beldon paused and then added, 'Val, I believe he stopped in your office first before heading upstairs. The portrait on the wall was crooked.'

'Looking for a safe?' Val hypothesised.

'Possibly. I have my conclusions.' Beldon rose and began to pace in front of the mantel. Lilya could see his brain working, all the pieces assembling into a coherent whole. 'There was no gift. If there had been and even if he'd thought it was acceptable to breach a lady's quarters to leave it, he would not have gone to the office first. I think there are some assumptions we may safely make. First, he was looking for something of value if he felt it might be kept in a safe. Second, it is something that Lilya uniquely possesses if he felt it would be in her room and not the others.'

Val nodded. 'The other bedrooms were not disturbed?'

'All the doors remained shut and he did not stop to check the room I saw him pass,' Beldon confirmed.

Lilya bit her lip. Beldon was only moments away from the truth. That meant she had only moments to think. What would she tell them? How could she tell the truth without lying *and* without involving them?

The arrival of the decanter bought her a few more minutes. Beldon and Val helped themselves to brandy and sipped thoughtfully. Philippa moved to sit beside her on the sofa, taking her hand comfortingly in her own. Lilya was glad for the support, even while she wished it wasn't necessary. Perhaps she should never have come here and put these lovely people at risk. But she couldn't waste time on regrets now. She had to think.

Then came the question Lilya had dreaded since the beginning of the conversation. 'Lilya, do you know what Christoph Agyros might be looking for?' It was Val who asked, but Beldon's question was far worse.

'What I want to know is why he could not approach you for it openly? He is clearly after something that has to be stolen.' Beldon's eyes were piercing, his tone hard. 'Lilya, what do you possess that you would not willingly give up if asked?'

It took all of her strength to meet his gaze. She wanted so badly to look away from that penetrating stare. In that moment she felt as if he saw all of her—that he knew without being told she had a secret.

There were no lies to tell. She could not lie to these people who had done everything for her. They'd given her a home. More importantly, they'd given her hope, what little there was to give. Lilya told the only truth she could offer them. 'I can't tell you.'

A quiet pandemonium settled on the room. She could hear the denials without them being spoken.

she was weak, utterly persuaded by his confidence that here was a man who could be her fortress. He'd fought Christoph unarmed. That small detail had not escaped her notice. Now her hero stood just inches from her.

'What is Christoph Agyros to you? Has he mis-used his position with you?' he asked.

'I think that's clear.' She kept her gaze firmly riv-eted on the dark, empty streets. She didn't dare look at him. 'He's a menace. He's shown that tonight.'

'He styled himself to be your suitor these last few weeks and you seemed to enjoy his company.'

'You and Val have determined those efforts were nothing more than subterfuge.'

'Still, Lilya, I would not tolerate him misusing you.'

She understood what he was asking in so many delicate words—had she harboured any feelings for the handsome foreigner?

'It hardly signifies. My heart cannot be engaged any longer.' There was a shred of hope here of avoid-ing other entanglements. Perhaps she could claim a broken heart and stave off any other contenders for the remainder of the Season. But it would be pretence only. She might have fancied the novelty of a coun-tryman, but she had not felt any personal affection for Christoph Agyros.

Understanding the situation from her perspective made Beldon's questions appear irrelevant. There were more important issues at stake than a broken heart. A chill crept over Lilya, suspicion blossoming. She put a hand on Beldon's arm out of reflex. 'You are not to challenge him to a duel, do you hear me?' Christoph was more dangerous than anyone could imagine. If he'd been here for the diamond, it meant the *Filiki Adamao* was here. Their resources ran deep and covert.

Beldon covered her hand with his where it rested on his arm, the usual excitement igniting most inconveniently even in the wake of this current crisis.

'Who are you protecting, Lilya? Me or him?' His voice was husky and low, highlighting the intimacy between them. There was no one around, the house was quiet.

'Us. I'm protecting all of us,' Lilya whispered.

'Your sentiment is noble, but unnecessary. Some of us do not need protecting.'

'And I am one of them,' Lilya said sternly.

'Meaning?' Beldon raised an elegant eyebrow in challenge. He knew very well what she meant.

'Meaning, *I* don't need a protector.' Certainly not him. She could easily care too much for this azure-eyed man who saw far too much about her than he should, stirred up feelings in her that she'd prefer to keep dormant.

He chuckled at her response. 'It's those who think they don't need help that need it the most.' He ran his thumb over the top of her hand, the light caress conjuring up a host of sensations. His voice was low and private, compelling. 'Lilya, let me help you.'

Temptation whispered, *Yes, let him. This is no untried boy full of ideals like Benjamin.* Here was a man her father would have admired. In the world of the Phanar, loyalty was the most valuable and often rarest commodity of all. A man lived and died by the strength of his friends and family.

Lilya stepped back, snatching back her hand from his grasp. She wanted distance. She sought it the only way she knew how. 'Perhaps now it's time for me to ask you what you mean by all this? What are you doing here, flirting with me with your touches and hot eyes when you intend to marry another? You talk of chivalry, but...'

Anger darkened Beldon's eyes, his jaw tightening. 'How dare you insinuate my honour is not all it should be? You know nothing about me. May I remind *you*, you were the one with a strange man upstairs seeking out her bedchamber.'

To think she'd almost fallen to the temptation moments ago. Lilya's temper snapped.

'And you're the one making love to me under the pretence of something else. You forget, Christoph Agyros has already tried to seduce the secret out of me.'

Beldon's voice became a growl, his eyes flashing. 'This is not love-making.' He stepped towards her and she backed up, her derrière hitting the wall. There was nowhere else to go.

Her chin went up in defiance. 'I will *not* be intimidated.'

But she wasn't immune to being other things she feared. Her pulse raced at his nearness. At this distance he was far more intoxicating than he'd ever been on the dance floor. The atmosphere between them had changed during the altercation, pregnant now with expectation, something explosive and potent was brewing, about to brim over.

A wicked glint lit his eyes. 'I don't mean to intimidate you, Lilya. I mean to kiss you.'

Chapter Eight

She started to make one last protest, but Beldon was far too swift. He tipped her chin up, his hand warm and strong where it cupped her cheek, his mouth on hers claiming a lover's kiss, the heat of his passion self-evident. It was all motion and response now, the opportunity for protest long past, not that she wanted to protest. Her lips parted to welcome him, his arms drew her close, letting the kiss deepen, their bodies involved in the interaction. She could feel the muscled hardness of him, the strength that was both physical and mental. One hand was in her hair, one at the small of her back, steadying her, guiding her.

She was vaguely aware of her own hands in his hair, of pressing her own body as close to his as she could, wanting desperately to fulfil this grow- ing need to be as close to him as possible. The kiss obliterated all else. There was no diamond, no secret, there was nothing but this.

But a kiss could not last for ever and when it was over all the same issues were still there plus some new ones; not the least was remembering to be angry.

'Don't think I don't see your intentions.'

'Oh?' he queried in aloof tones, allowing her to step around him.

'Christoph Agyros did not succeed in seducing my secret out of me and neither will you.' Feelings a-jumble and head held high, with all the aplomb she could manage Lilya sailed towards the door.

Laughter of a friendly sort trailed after her. 'Lilya,' Beldon's voice called out, halting her hopefully magnificent departure. She turned at the doorway.

'You make me smile.' Beldon grinned, arms crossed, powerful body lounging against one of Philippa's prized pillars. A potent thrill of desire shot through her at the sight.

Magnificent departure ruined.

She had to say something. He absolutely could *not* have the last word, not tonight. 'You make me crazy.'

'I know.'

His good-natured laughter followed her up the stairs.

How dare he kiss her, how dare he laugh at her,

how dare he…? Well, that list could go on and on. Best stop or she'd never get to sleep.

Lilya dressed for bed alone, unwilling to wake her maid. There was too much to think about. There was the diamond and then there was Beldon. They were going to be the death of her unless she acted quickly.

She sat up in her favourite chair by the window. What did Christoph really know? Did he know with a certainty she had the diamond or was he guessing? England was a long way from the Balkans, an expensive journey for a wild-goose hunt.

The *Filiki Adamao* would be getting desperate. The London talks were dividing up borders, determining the boundaries of the new Greek state. The three great powers would be casting about for a new king next. If the *Filiki* meant to be the puppet masters behind the throne, they'd have to act quickly and secure the diamond as their collateral to power. It was not out of the realm of possibility that the *Filiki* was tracking down all possible suspects, casting their net wide in order to catch something, anything.

These considerations begged other questions. Should she approach Christoph directly and ask him? Then try to persuade him that she didn't have the diamond? The idea was quickly discarded. If she knew of the diamond, it made her culpable. She would not be asking of something she did not have.

Lilya thought of her dagger. Perhaps in disguise as a man, she could threaten the truth out of him, catch him unawares in a dark alley. Also, too dangerous. If he opted not to be scared, she had no way to overpower him. Her strength was no match for a man trained to danger.

The thought summoned Beldon to mind. If she wanted to approach Christoph in any way, she needed an ally. Beldon had proven himself Christoph's equal tonight, maybe more. Beldon certainly hadn't looked the worse for wear. He hadn't kissed like it either. Clearly Christoph hadn't landed any punches in the jaw.

Lilya gave up the chair for the bed and crawled between the cool sheets. Did she dare risk Beldon's involvement? What had the kiss meant? They'd been angry, feelings high. Perhaps the kiss hadn't meant anything more than misplaced emotions. But she could not discard the kiss so easily. She could not pretend there'd been nothing between them. The sharp awareness tonight had sprung between them before.

She also could not ignore the fact that no matter what had sparked the kiss, she'd liked it. Quite a lot. Lilya hugged her pillow to her. Now she knew why women looked over their fans at him, why they followed him around ballrooms with their eyes. Beldon Stratten could kiss a woman into oblivion, could make her forget everything, could turn her brains to porridge and her insides to jelly.

Ah, yes, Lilya sighed. Now she knew. And she

rather wished she didn't. She was starting to rethink everything, her thoughts peppered with 'maybes' and 'what ifs'. What if Beldon could safely be enlisted to her cause, what if Christoph did know absolutely about the diamond, then it might be possible to…to what? Let herself fall in love with Beldon? Live a normal life, whatever or wherever that might be?

There were darker 'what ifs', too. What if Christoph knew she had it? What if Beldon was hurt because of her? *Then* she should run as far from England as she could and never look back, but running wouldn't save her. In time, Christoph or someone else would hunt her down. But running would save the people she loved: Val and Philippa, Constantine and Val's little boy, and even though she didn't want to admit it to herself, that list included Beldon.

Not a pleasant choice to fall asleep by.

Everything looks better by morning light. Whoever said that was wrong. *Definitely wrong.* Lilya knew it the moment she awoke. The possibilities of the night were full of glaring improbabilities in the bright light of morning.

Last night she'd been kissing Beldon and believing her previously established limitations might be just that—limitations. Perhaps she could have a happy-ever-after, after all. His kisses were a fool's ambrosia coming on the heels of the night's reality: Christoph Agyros had come hunting her and the diamond and he hadn't come alone. He was not a maverick operating by himself. He was a representative of a larger cartel. Beldon might think Agyros could be managed. But he did not understand—Agyros was one of many, merely a single head on the hydra. Beldon saw only the individual man.

Her maid, Sally, swept into the room with fresh linens, cheery and oblivious to Lilya's dilemma. Lilya threw her blankets over her head and groaned. She wanted to stay in bed. If she got up and dressed, she'd have to go downstairs and face them all.

'Would you like me to lay out your lavender dress with the violet ribbons?' Sally threw open the wardrobe; Lilya could hear the left hinge squeak. Lilya grumbled her assent. Lavender was as good a colour as any to face the day with.

Val and Philippa were already at breakfast when she arrived. Philippa greeted her cheerfully and Val's plate was piled with his customary eggs and ham. It might have been an ordinary day in the viscount's household with everyone trying their best to put a good face on the revelations of the prior evening.

But there was only so much a sunny disposition could hide. A man hurried into the breakfast room to speak with Val. Val murmured a few words and sent him on his way. Lilya glanced from Philippa to Valerian, looking for an explanation.

Philippa set down her fork. 'He's one of the men

Val has posted outside the town house. He—*we*,' Philippa corrected, 'felt it was necessary for all our safety.'

Guards. Lilya's stomach plummeted. She'd turned the lovely town house into a fortress, not just for herself but for them, too. But she could not argue against the precautions. She could not protest that Val was overreacting. Val had no idea what he was protecting against, but his instincts were right. The fear of the previous night resurfaced; she ought not to have come here.

She had just sat down with a modest plate of toast and eggs when Beldon entered the room. He filled his plate and sat across from her.

'How are you this morning, Lilya?' he enquired.

'I am well,' she answered tentatively, hating how her eyes drifted to his mouth, the mouth that had kissed her.

Would it always be this way from now on? Would she be able to have a conversation with him without thinking of his lips? He forked a bite of egg and she blushed. She'd been doing it again. His mouth quirked into the quickest of grins.

He knew.

Her mortification was complete.

'We must go about our day as normally as possible,' Valerian was saying when she dragged her thoughts back to the conversation. 'The guards are dressed in plain clothing with the hopes that Christoph might not be alert to them immediately. I'd like nothing better than to see the bounder attempt to force an entry.'

That would mean an interrogation. If Christoph were caught, Beldon and Val would question him personally and then they would know about the diamond. They wouldn't have to wait for her to share the secret.

Lilya took a last bite of eggs and pushed her plate away, most of her food untouched. 'If you'll excuse me, please?' She had to think, somewhere away from all these politely prying eyes of the people she loved. How could she protect them when they had so boldly rushed into danger on her behalf? They'd engaged the fight without knowing what they fought against.

She sought out a small, quiet room at the back of the house. It was filled with morning sun and had been intended for use by the lady of the house as an office. But it went unused by anyone except her since Philippa preferred to keep her own desk in Valerian's office.

Lilya curled up on the sofa, letting the abundance of morning light bathe her face. She closed her eyes against its brightness and sought clarity. All she had feared was coming to pass *without* her secret being known. Valerian's family and Beldon were already involved. In hindsight, she could see that they'd been involved the moment she'd arrived. Her very presence involved them, secret or not. Keeping knowledge of the diamond from them wouldn't protect them any longer. In fact, keeping them unaware might even put them at a grave disadvantage. They could only defend against so many circumstances without specific knowledge.

Lilya sighed. She would have to tell them or leave unaccountably and without explanation.

'Are you all right?'

Lilya's eyes flew open, her body starting at the intrusion. 'I'm fine.' She turned to see Beldon striding towards her, his presence filling the small room. He looked entirely masculine amid the feminine setting of pink-and-yellow chintz.

'You did not seem fine at breakfast,' Beldon challenged, taking seat beside her.

'There is a lot to think about.'

Beldon reached out to cover her hand where it lay in her lap. 'You don't have to do this alone,' he began.

Lilya shook her head and snatched her hand way. 'We've done this vignette before. Don't touch me. It will just make things worse, as we learned last night.'

She needed space. She sought the security of the French doors leading out into a private garden, but Beldon followed her.

'How does it make anything worse?' They were alone in the garden except for the lone tweet of a bird in the hedge.

'I usually admire persistence, Beldon. But not

in this case.' Lilya fingered the soft edges of a rose petal, deliberately keeping her tone cool and her back to him. Maybe if she needled him, angered him enough, he'd go away. He would hate her soon enough as it was. Once her secret was further defined, he'd despise her for coming here, for dragging them unsuspecting and without permission into her dark world of secrets. There would be no more kisses or tender glances then.

Her strategy erred greatly. Beldon *was* angered, but it had the reverse effect. Instead of leaving, Beldon advanced, gripping her shoulder and spinning her around. 'Look at me, Lilya. I grant that you do not know me well. However, in the time you *have* known me, have I ever been a man who runs from trouble? Have I ever been a man who has abandoned his friends in their hour of need? You cannot expect me to do less for you.' Anger born of passion fired his words. It was positively mesmerising and true.

His words were not a meaningless oratory of bravado. This man had fought beside Valerian when men had come to arrest him on charges of treason. This man had used every resource at his disposal to keep watch over Val while he was in Newgate awaiting trial. This man had not abandoned Val in his most desperate hour.

Lilya had admired him during those difficult days, a staunch support to Philippa and to herself, a newly arrived stranger. Now, he pledged that same intense loyalty to her and it was entirely tempting to take it. Only the consequences of what it would mean to him held her in any kind of check. She would not see him dead on the altar of his own chivalry.

'You only say this because you don't know what you're up against,' Lilya countered.

'I want to know. I would know, if you would tell me. But if you won't, then I'll fight blindly.'

'That's not something I can let you do.'

Beldon's frustration peaked. 'I will not be protected through ignorance, Lilya. You do not protect me at all with this display of stubbornness.' He was working hard to keep his temper in check. His hands clenched and unclenched at his sides, his shoulders drawn in tension. Beldon sank on to a stone bench, his agitated hands pushing through his hair, leaving it disarmingly dishevelled.

His voice was calmer when he spoke again. 'If you won't listen to reason, Lilya, maybe you'll listen to a story.' He gestured to the seat next to him on the bench and she sat gingerly, not wanting to be persuaded, but not able to resist the lure.

'Lilya, people have tried to protect me before from unpleasantness. Those manoeuvres failed miserably and with great cost, not only to me but to those around me—Valerian and Philippa specifically.' He looked up at her with a rueful smile. 'Oblivion and ignorance are not protection, not *true* protection. My father believed they were.' He reached a hand out for her.

'My father was a good man. He loved his family and he was generous to a fault. I mean that literally. We had a respectable fortune and it was spent on providing us the best of everything: expensive schools, fine horses, beautiful clothes and jewels for my mother. But when the war came and our income changed, my father could not bear to make the adjustments. By the time the war was over and economic depression had set in, the Pendennys coffers were barely functional. To compound matters, some of our mines were depleted. The little things first: seldom-worn jewels, expensiv around the house. Then bigger item house was stripped down to its ba the horses and the carriage. We kept ride, but it was nothing compared to housed fifteen grand steeds. Philipp go.' He paused. 'That's right. Philippa her first marriage to the magnificent Marquis of Cambourne. Then Val went. He and Philippa were young and desperately in love. He couldn't stay and watch her become the wife of another. But what could he do? If he married her, he doomed the Pendennyses to poverty. There was too much honour in him to do that. By the time I was twenty-one, I'd lost everything, including my sister and my best friend.' His tone was harsh and bitter.

This bit of news stunned Lilya. She had not heard this part of the Pendennys history. Philippa had certainly not alluded to any of this in the time she'd been here.

'The worst of it was,' Beldon went on, 'I didn't understand the reason for any of it until it was too late. I was away at school, a very expensive school, I might add, and then my father kept me in London at the Pendennys town house with an allowance. I was ignorant of all that had been sacrificed. I saw only Philippa and her beautiful gowns in town for her Season. I think Philippa was not quite aware either. Even Valerian had been corralled by my father to keep the worst of it from me. I knew there was a general economic depression, but when I asked about our family finances, I was told things were under control, if a little tight. My father was always jovial when he said it as if a few bills were of no real consequence. And why should they be? We'd always had plenty. Money was a fluid and replenishable commodity. My father died a year after Philippa married Cambourne. That was when I discovered part of the Pendennys debt.

'At the time, I thought it was fortuitous Cambourne was on hand. Without his loan, I could never have diversified our holdings and start to claw my way back to financial security.' He looked meaningfully at Lilya. 'It wasn't until Valerian returned after his nine-year absence that I discovered Philippa had been married to Cambourne for his money on purpose. My father had traded her for funds.'

Beldon gave a wry smile. 'She came to like and respect Cambourne and he adored his young wife. It wasn't a bad marriage, but it wasn't her choice. She had loved Valerian from the start and he loved her, but all that had been set aside for me.'

Lilya felt Beldon's grip tighten. 'I was the heir, I was to be protected at all costs so that I might live the life my father imagined for me, the wealthy scion. It wasn't until Val came home that I knew all that had been done to protect me from it.'

'And so you've spent the last ten years of your life putting the estate to rights,' Lilya finished softly for him. This part of the story she knew. Beldon had devoted himself selflessly to the restoration of the Pendennys estate. Every pound of every investment had gone into improving the estate he'd become so proud of. She thought she understood now why he'd waited to marry. He wanted to avoid the well-meant sins of his father, making sure the coffers were ready for a family and a wife.

'It's why I won't stand by and be so blindly "protected" again.' There was a resolute fierceness edging his voice. 'Not by you or anyone else I care for.'

He cared for her. In that statement the core of Beldon Stratten was revealed, a man who held family and honour dearest of all. It was a good reason to love him, although the fact that he kissed like sin itself was a powerful recommendation, too. Perhaps that was the hour in which she first fell.

'Wait here. There's something I want to show you.' Lilya raced upstairs before she could change her mind.

Chapter Nine

'You want to show me a hat box?'

'Open it.' She thrust the box at him, her words coming out in a rush. She was breathless from her run and more than a little worried about his reaction. What would he think when he saw it? When she told him? She'd run through the house, not caring who saw her for fear her thoughts might catch up with her, that she might change her mind before she could put the box in Beldon's hands.

Beldon opened the lid, his gaze alternating between her and the box, grim and searching. His hands delved into the tissue and Lilya instinctively stepped back, her hands finding the door and shutting it firmly behind her. She'd never shown *Adamao* to anyone, not even Val and Philippa.

She knew the moment he'd found the diamond.

His hand closed around the smooth glassy surface of it. His eyes narrowed, his mind racing to assess the contents in his hand before he withdrew it from the box, trying to guess what he'd found. He pulled it out and stared.

'What is this, Lilya?' His voice was a grim mixture of awe and horror, part of him already piecing together conclusions.

'It's a diamond.'

Beldon lifted the gem to the light, letting its facets reflect prisms on to the walls and fall. 'I know that. But it's not just any diamond. I've never seen one of this cut and colour before.'

'It's a pink diamond, very rare. I don't know of any others on record. It's 52 carats.' She knew it by rote.

Beldon gave her a considering look. 'This is what Agyros is after, isn't it?'

She nodded. Beldon's features went hard and she wished for a moment she could have lied. She could see his thoughts in his eyes. 'It's not just Christoph,' she hurried on, 'there's a secret society, the *Filiki Adamao*, that's been searching for the diamond since its supposed disappearance four hundred years ago.'

Beldon gave her one of his incredulous, raised-eyebrow stares. While large by gem standards, the diamond seemed insignificant in Beldon's hand compared to the problems associated with it. He replaced the diamond into the depths of the hat box and put the lid on. 'Four hundred years? Has it always been with your family?'

'Yes. My father passed it to me the day before his execution,' she said quietly, taking the diamond from Beldon. She was secretly amazed that he'd given it up so readily. She didn't think Christoph Agyros would have. 'After the fall of Constantinople in 1453, the Phanar elders decreed the diamond too great of temptation to our community. They entrusted it to our care. We are to keep it secret for the safety of the Phanar. Greed is a most dangerous temptation.'

'But the *Filiki Adamao* has not believed that story, that the diamond has been lost,' Beldon mused. 'Do they think the diamond will buy them the monarchy?'

She could see Beldon thought the idea slightly outrageous. A single jewel, rare as it was, for a crown? 'Of course they do; the Three Powers think they can buy the throne for sixty billion francs. It is no different.'

'So this *Filiki Adamao* think to be the power behind the throne?' Beldon's mind worked fast to assimilate the implications.

Lilya nodded. 'Especially now since Leopold of Belgium has refused the throne and Europe is casting about for another kingly candidate.'

'There is talk the throne will be offered to Prince Otto of Bavaria,' Beldon put in.

Lilya shrugged, unimpressed. 'He's a mere child.

Things are more precarious now than ever. Leopold's refusal has left a vacuum of power. Men are watching and waiting for the chance to fill it. The *Filiki* must move now before loose ends are sewn up if they wish to influence the new Greece. If they had the diamond, they could buy a king like Otto, control him. That assumes they want a king at all.'

'You think they don't?' She heard his doubt. His was a rational, political mind.

'No, it is not clear to me that the *Filiki Adamao* prefer a king or even independence. Without a king, perhaps they could be in charge as they were in the golden age of Phanar. They do not need a throne to have power.' History was full of examples of people who ruled without the benefit of a crown; bankers, diplomats, advisors who skillfully guided policies.

'I do not think a diamond could do all that.' Beldon shook his head sceptically.

Lilya offered a wry smile. 'It could if you consider this: *Adamao*'s appeal isn't all about its financial worth. Translated, *Adamao* means "I tame" or perhaps in an older version of the language, "I subdue". There are those who believe the myth-history surrounding it. Adamao is believed to have been worn by Helen of Troy when she eloped with Paris. Some say Paris stole Helen not for her beauty alone but for the jewel itself because it brought extraordinary good luck and prosperity to those who possessed it.'

'And you've had such extraordinarily good luck with it in your possession,' Beldon said drily.

'Well, I cannot say I've experienced the diamond's purported powers firsthand,' Lilya answered with a smile, thankful for the relief his brief humour brought. For all the good luck it was reputed to bring, the diamond had brought plenty of despair in the wake of men's attempts to acquire the jewel for themselves. If one believed the myths, one had only to look to the Trojan War for verification.

Beldon stood up and paced the length of the small room. 'What is all this to you, Lilya? Do you care so much for the independence of Greece? You were a child when the wars began and, in truth, you're little more than that now.'

The last fired her temper. 'Little more than a child? What is this to me?' she flared, anger and disappointment swamping her. She'd hoped for more from Beldon. She had trusted him with her great secret. 'My brother Alexei was little more than a child when Ottoman soldiers cut him down at Negush.'

'Yes, but that wasn't about the diamond. It was not the *Filiki Adamao* that massacred your people,' Beldon interrupted.

'No, it wasn't,' Lilya responded sharply. 'That was about quelling independence. What is going on now is about independence, too. Freedom is linked to the diamond. The Phanariot elders knew the hazards of the diamond. They rightly feared it could be used to create a tyranny. It's too much power for any one man or any one group to wield.'

'You have to tell Val and Philippa.' Beldon sat down and pushed his hands through his hair. 'Then we can decide what to do.'

Lilya shook her head. 'I will tell them. But there will be no "we" deciding what to do. If there's any doing of anything, it will be by me alone.' She had to be firm on this point. *She* would take the risks, no one else. 'Telling Val and Philippa is for their own safety. I am not telling them as a ploy for enlisting their help, or yours.'

'Don't be stubborn, Lilya. Let us help. You are only one woman against an unseen enemy.'

It was not the right thing to say. Lilya stopped him with a cold glare. 'Yes, I am and I have made it this far. Now, if you'll excuse me?'

Beldon sprawled against the cushions of the dainty sofa. Last night, Lilya's sharp wit had been enjoyable. This morning it was merely sharp, and sharp things, as a rule, hurt when one was stabbed with them. He had no doubt she was telling Valerian and Philippa right now what she'd already told him. She'd wanted to do it alone. She had too much pride. She'd not want it to look as if she'd made this decision because of his prompting.

He would let her have her privacy and her pride.

He needed time to think, time to sort through all she'd shared. Ultimately, he needed time to determine what his role in this was to be. Beldon was well aware that his role didn't have to be a role at all. Other than his role as brother-in-law to her guardian, he need do nothing more than nod his head and offer her verbal support and go about his own pursuits in town.

But she'd become one of those pursuits over the past few weeks. If he chose to do nothing about the diamond, that pursuit would have to end before it even became official. The thought of not dancing, not conversing, not occasionally sparring with her and certainly not stealing the rare kiss from her did not sit well with him.

Beldon knew he must tread carefully and honestly with himself here. He'd defended her twice against Christoph's less-honourable intentions by intervening in the garden and again with the fisticuffs last night. Were those simply the acts of a gentleman doing his duty or were they motivated by something more? If so, what was that something more? It was daunting to give a name to the passion invited by their kiss. Lilya had been all fire in his arms, igniting like dry tinder at his touch. His body had answered in kind. The attraction was mutual.

More importantly, if he chose a larger role in her life, what would he do? What *could* he do? Lilya made it clear that Christoph was just one head of the

Filiki Adamao hydra. There would be others. Lilya's shocking disclosures this morning had made it clear the kind of perils she lived in at all times regardless of war or peace.

That was long-term thinking, however. There was still the present situation to deal with. Christoph Agyros suspected she had the diamond and he was at large, able to pursue his mission. He was both devious and arrogantly dangerous. He would not hesitate to threaten Lilya outright or indiscreetly.

By rights and logic, the situation begged him to distance himself. Lilya and her secrets threatened all he'd worked for. She could not be the wife he'd come to London looking for. But the longer he thought on all she'd told him, the more his admiration grew. He understood the significance of what she'd shared, and also the significance of what had gone unsaid; what the diamond meant for her life. He'd heard the unspoken remorse when she'd talked of her father and Alexei. The charge was not to have come to her. It should have gone to Alexei, the oldest male. She would have been free of the responsibility but his death at Negush and her father's execution had changed all that.

She had not chosen to be tied to the diamond, it had simply come to her. Beldon understood, too, she was bound by more than a political legacy. She was bound to the charge by familial loyalty, which was to her, perhaps, a more powerful bond than any political tie. To fail the charge would be to fail her father. Lilya was caught neatly in a web spun long before her birth and Beldon found he did not want to leave her there alone.

'Lord Pendennys, you're wanted in the study.' A footman interrupted his thoughts with the summons. Lilya must be done telling them. Val would want to lay plans now. Good, Beldon had a few plans of his own to offer.

'I should go,' Lilya said as he stepped into the study. 'If I leave quickly, Christoph will not be able to follow. I'll have a few days' lead on him.'

'Absolutely not.' Beldon shut the door behind him with more force than intended. 'You're not going anywhere.' He understood what had precipitated her flight from her homeland but those running days were over. She had him now, and Val and Philippa, too.

Lilya's chin went up in stubborn defiance. 'It is the only way. I've told you the kind of men who hunt this diamond. They are not to be toyed with. They've devoted their lives to the pursuit. They will not stop until they're convinced the diamond has passed out of history.'

Beldon exchanged a long-suffering look with Valerian. Apparently this wasn't the first time in the conversation she'd voiced this idea.

'Perhaps we can help her get away to a place

where she won't have to run again,' Philippa put in from her chair, uncharacteristically pale.

'Philippa is right,' Lilya protested. 'I am a danger to your family. It's not fair to have you all in fear because of me. Val, you must think of your little son and of my brother, Constantine. Agyros or some other in the future will come for them in order to get to me. If I disappear, you are no more use to him. The *Filiki* will not waste time on dead ends. It is why they've left me alone for so long.' She shot a meaningful glance Beldon's direction 'They thought as you did that a woman couldn't possibly be the guardian of the diamond.'

Beldon took the chair next to Philippa. 'I can see I'll be apologising for that remark several times over. My poor choice of words aside, you simply can't leave, Lilya. Leaving will confirm his suspicions. You would only run if you had the diamond and knew why he'd come.'

'But staying corners me. We cannot live in a guarded town house for ever. If Agyros thinks we have hired protection, that, too, will raise his suspicions,' Lilya countered, her dark eyes flashing with temper over being countermanded.

'Beldon's right. The guards are all plainly clothed and unobtrusive. We can call them off. What we need is a strategy that will keep you here and dissuade Christoph from the notion that you have the diamond.' Val drummed long fingers on the desk top. He offered Lilya a commiserating smile. 'Too bad you couldn't just be a normal society miss, my dear.'

'Why not?' Philippa sat forwards, some new energy overriding her earlier fears for her young family. 'Why not be a normal débutante? What does a normal young society miss want? A round of parties, pretty dresses, a proposal, a wedding. Lilya has all of that in place already.'

'Except for the proposal part,' Beldon put in.

'Don't you see?' Philippa divided her gaze between him and her husband. Beldon was glad to see Val was as perplexed as he was, the mysteries of the feminine mind being what they were.

Philippa plunged ahead. 'If Lilya had the diamond, marriage would be the last thing on her mind. Marriage is permanent. She'd be dragging a husband into this web of intrigue and later children. Marriage anchors her to England. She could not run any more, which is hardly what the keeper of the diamond would want.

'Marriage to a peer is public. If Lilya had the diamond, the last thing she'd do is flaunt her whereabouts with a large wedding, announcements in the paper and taking her place in society as a hostess. She'd never be able to conceal herself. The best part is, the stage is already laid. She's in London, she's here under her own name, and she's already being courted by all the right sorts of men with titles and positions. There's been no pretence of hiding. If an engagement is announced, if a wedding is held, it won't look awkward or contrived. It will be the natural outcome of a lovely, well-dowered young woman going to London.'

'No, the only awkward part would be the part where there's no groom at the wedding.' Beldon chuckled. 'But perhaps part of the plan could work, Val? What do you think of the old "hide in plain sight" strategy?'

Val looked at his wife, contemplating the plan. 'I think it would work, but we have to go all the way. Agyros is already here and suspicious. Only a marriage will dissuade him. It's the choice to anchor herself in England that matters. That's what sells this plan. If there's no anchor, the option to run still exists, and if she can run, she'll always be a suspect.'

Lilya stood up so quickly her chair wobbled, threatening to fall back from the force of her rising. 'I will not stand here and be talked about as if I'm not in the room.' She shot Val and Beldon lethal looks. 'Running is the only choice. There are three reasons why.' She proceeded to count them off on her fingers. 'First, I could not burden an unsuspecting husband. Second, even if one of my suitors came up to scratch, it wouldn't be fast enough. No one is likely to offer until July and we need a husband now, or at least an engagement to announce. Third, I refuse on principle to live a lie and it might not even work.'

She was magnificent in her anger, Beldon thought, something lusty and rebellious stirring in his lower parts. He wanted to kiss her into compliance until their bodies overruled their minds and they forgot their differences: her secret, his search for the 'perfect' wife.

'The marquis's son could be brought up to scratch sooner than that, I am certain of it, and perhaps he could be told...' Philippa was saying.

The image of giving Lilya to the marquis's son was reprehensible. Simply giving her to another must not be tolerated, his body argued.

'No.' The words were out of his mouth before his mind could make his body take them back. 'Lilya will marry me.'

Chapter Ten

Lilya blanched and blindly groped for the chair she'd nearly toppled. 'I'm not going to marry anyone and I'm certainly not going to marry someone who hasn't asked me.' In his high-handed way, he'd announced it to the room. As proposals went, it was definitely not the stuff of dreams. Nightmares, perhaps.

'Yes, you are, because it makes sense, because it protects you and your quest.' Beldon was all cold logic, his eyes holding hers in a challenging stare. 'I will "come up to scratch" immediately. We can have an announcement in *The Times* by tomorrow morning. I will not be an unsuspecting husband.' He paused, his eyes glinting with something wicked. 'And finally, you won't be living a lie with me. I can give you a good life and we have already established we have, shall we say, a certain amount of mutual esteem for one another?'

'What exactly have you been doing with my ward, Beldon? You were supposed to be her chaperon, not the one she needed chaperoning from,' Valerian broke in.

'It hardly signifies now that we're getting married. I'll have the announcement penned tonight, Val.'

'Wait!' Lilya cried. In all her imaginings, in all her fantasies of marrying Beldon, it had never been like this. He was surrendering himself on the altar of matrimony. She wanted a husband, not a sacrifice. This was miserable.

Philippa rose and slipped her arm through Lilya's. 'Come, dear, the gentlemen have things to discuss and so do we. We must decide on a dress and flowers.'

'I haven't agreed to anything...' Lilya sputtered. Didn't anyone else see how miserable this was? This was happening too fast. The very thing she wanted to avoid, marriage, had suddenly become her lifeline in a scheme so crazy that it might work.

Philippa's reasoning was sound. Agyros would be put off by the permanence of her choice. Lilya saw the necessity for a quick wedding, too. Marriage to someone else made it impossible for Agyros to marry her himself.

But just because the plan had merit didn't mean she liked it. She'd never wanted Beldon this way and

happily engaged couple, the epitome of two people caught up in a whirlwind courtship.

Beldon stood beside her in their corner of the ball-room, playing the pleased prospective bridegroom to the hilt as he accepted congratulations from those who passed by them. 'We have not yet decided where to hold the wedding. I would love to marry in Corn-wall, but my bride prefers a large wedding here in town at St George's.' He shot her a look of besotted indulgence.

'I most certainly do *not*,' Lilya hissed after the couple moved on. 'I'd prefer no wedding at all, as you well know.'

The hard look Beldon gave her was positive-ly frigid, far from the gaze of warm tolerance he'd feigned moments earlier. 'I am well aware of your desires. You've made sure of that. However, I am not convinced that marriage to me is worse than death at the hands of your various and invisible enemies.'

'That's because you're not a recipient of your own high-handed arrogance,' Lilya muttered, her temper getting the better of her.

'What is that—?' Beldon pasted on a smile and bowed, breaking off his comment in mid-sentence. 'Good evening, Mrs Greenward. Yes, I'm elated with my good fortune. Thank you so much.' The smile faded, the conversation resumed. '—supposed to mean exactly?'

'I never asked to be rescued. I never asked for a

hero or a sacrifice. I am perfectly fine on my own. I don't owe you for this.'

Beldon glared, a thought flitting across the planes of his face. Then he gripped her arm and pulled her through the ballroom.

'Where are we going?' Lilya protested.

'Outside' was growled through gritted teeth. He led them to a quiet bench near the far fence of the garden. 'There, now we can talk.'

'I don't want to marry you,' Lilya began, but Beldon cut her off with a strong look.

'Wait, I lied. When I said now we can talk, I meant I could talk and you could listen. I am more than clear on your position regarding our upcoming nuptials. But there is no other way to dissuade him—'

'There's no guarantee this will work,' Lilya interrupted.

'You don't listen very well, do you?' Beldon's eyes were dangerously dark. 'We might as well try this. Running won't work at all except to get yourself followed. That can hardly be what you wish.'

'And marriage *is* what I wish?'

Exasperation was evident on his features. 'Stop pretending you aren't attracted to me, Lilya. You'll like being married to me. You've been flirting with me since we met.'

'I beg your pardon. I hardly know you when all is said and done.' She rose up, trying for a dignified exit, trying to hide the truth behind a façade of offended hurt. She probably would like being married to him in some regards, if their kiss was any indicator. 'For the record, I have not been flirting. If anyone's been flirting, it's been you,' she shot back. 'With your hand kissing, and touching my arm just so, and—' She broke off.

'You mean like this?' His voice was low and private, sending a warm thrill straight to her belly as his finger traced light circles on the back of her gloved hand. 'And like this?' His hand moved up her arm in a feathery touch that sent all nature of skittering delights shooting through her. His fingers found the tiny buttons of her long glove, deftly slipping them through their loops, but his eyes were riveted on her face, not once looking at the progress of his hands. His eyes darkened to the shade of midnight as he peeled the glove down her wrist.

'Imagine what I could do to that gown of yours,' he whispered, removing the last of the glove.

A delicious tremor took her as his lips found the inside of her wrist, her mind wild with vivid conjurings, of his hands on more than her glove, his mouth on more than her wrist, of his hands on her shoulders, pushing down her gown until she was bared before him. He pressed a kiss to the palm of her hand and a gasp of pleasure escaped her.

She was supposed to resist this, but it was so hard. Who'd have thought it would be like this? No one had ever told her a kiss, a mere touch, could render her senseless to the dangers of her world. It was much harder to resist the temptations of love once she'd experienced them than to resist the unknown. She hadn't known what she was giving up.

She tugged, but Beldon was unwilling to let her go. 'You haven't forgotten our kiss, have you?' Helplessly, she shook her head. He was drawing her close again, close to his strength, the power of his body, the power of surrender. His lips found her mouth, already parted, already begging for him whether she willed it or not. His tongue played sensuously along her bottom lip and she gave herself over to the delights he promised. Resistance was futile, for the moment. And, for the moment, that was fine with her.

In his arms, she could pretend a great many things. Passion was not one of them—that was genuine. Oh Lord, that was genuine. He was in her mouth now, teasing and tempting, the sweet taste of after-supper brandy lingering on his tongue, and she was pressed to him, revelling in the hard masculine planes of him. His mouth trailed kisses down her throat, a hand moving to gather up the fullness of her skirts until she could feel the warm night air on her thighs. She gasped at the decadence he'd awakened in her.

'You rouse to me, Lilya. There's no shame in it,' he murmured, husky tones indicating she was not the only one aroused. His hand swept up the curve of her leg and halted.

'What do we have here?'

Her dagger. She'd forgotten, entirely.

He ably removed the dagger from the sheath and held it to the dim light, his eyes meeting hers, glinting as dangerously as the sharp edge of her knife.

The passion ebbed.

'The diamond is not a game.' How she wished it was. How she wished she could reach out and claim the man who stood before her, the remnants of their interlude evident in his ragged breath, his rumpled hair. Had she done that? She hadn't realised... How she wished Beldon had proposed to her out of love, that he'd kissed her for a reason other than to make a point. Passion was powerful, but it wasn't love and she was not foolish enough to mistake it.

'I never thought it was,' Beldon answered grimly, passing the blade back to her. 'You won't need this after we marry. *I'll* protect you then, with my name, and, if necessary, with my body.'

Such powerful words. An irrational thrill of hope rose within her; hope that this time it could be different, hope that perhaps there was something more behind his offer of marriage than duty. Hope that she wasn't on the brink of repeating her father's mistakes. A little bit of hope went a long way.

She'd meant to persuade him to call off the engagement tonight. Instead, he'd been the one to do the convincing. She let him lead her back inside on to the dance floor and into the familiar patterns of a waltz. She understood what returning to the ballroom meant. It meant their engagement was implicitly sealed. There would be no backing out now. It meant she believed. In him. Oh God, how she wanted to believe in this broad-shouldered man whose aloof demeanour hid an extraordinary capacity for passion, whose commitment to right demanded an adherence to duty and honour at any cost. Most of all, she wanted to believe her folly would not see him dead.

Chapter Eleven

She didn't believe him! It galled him to the very core of his being as a gentleman. Even the morning after the Forthby ball he found her lack of trust maddening. A night's sleep hadn't changed that. He'd pledged his protection and she had not believed he could deliver it. He'd seen it in her eyes even as she gave evidence to the contrary.

Beldon heaped a plate full of sausages and toast and sat down in the breakfast room of Pendennys House. The town house was quiet after his brief tenure at Valerian's, perhaps too quiet. Here, he was the only resident. A glance at the wall clock told him they'd all be sitting down to breakfast over there, too. At Val's there'd be chatter at the table. Philippa would be discussing politics with Val or the daily social calendar with Lilya, or perhaps the wedding.

His wedding.

He'd come to London to find a wife. Technically, he supposed he'd accomplished his goal. He'd not imagined it happening this way or with Lilya of all people, but he'd be going home with a wife, the next Lady Pendennys, the mother of his children, the co-keeper of his dreams. He hoped Lilya was up to it. Truth was, he just didn't know. He'd always thought he'd know, that it would be clear that he'd chosen well.

The last thing he'd thought he'd do was choose impulsively, throwing his vaunted criteria to the proverbial winds. But when the moment had come, he had recognised with a sudden clarity he knew he could not give her up to another for the simple expediency of outwitting Christoph Agyros. And she would not have settled for anyone else. He'd seen it in her eyes. She'd meant it when she'd said she wouldn't implicate an unwitting husband in the plot. If it had been any other man, she would have run. So he'd offered himself. But his offering was not purely selfless. She fired his blood like no other, arousing him, challenging him, meeting him as an equal in all ways both mentally and physically. Her sense of honour went as deeply as his. She understood the importance of family. And she was honest in her passion. Just remembering their heated encounter in the Forthby garden was enough to cause the stir-rings of his arousal. She'd been liquid fire in his arms, melting into him, igniting beneath his touch even though that hadn't been her intention. He knew precisely what she'd meant to do in the garden when he'd dragged her from the ballroom, and it hadn't been kissing him. She'd meant to get him to break the engagement.

It was something of a victory that she hadn't even got close to succeeding with her gambit. But it was only a partial victory. She believed in the dagger strapped to her thigh more than she believed in his abilities to protect her. Admittedly, there was something deliciously arousing about a woman with a dagger beneath her skirts, but he didn't want his wife, his *woman*, to ever have to actually use it. A woman should be safe with her man.

And Lilya would be. Even now, the ploy was working.

Agyros had disappeared from society events since the night he'd been caught upstairs at Val's. Still, Beldon was a cautious man. He didn't mean to be far from Lilya's side until he could slip a ring on her finger. The sooner they were married the better. Marriage would not only remove her from Agyros's clutches and the threat of forced elopement, it would also offer her the legal protection of his name. Beldon pushed back from the table, making plans for his day. He'd stop by Val's and see if Lilya wanted to go to Hatchard's. It was as good a reason as any for keeping her close.

* * *

An hour later, he helped Lilya into his phaeton after promising Philippa to have her to the dressmaker's in time for a fitting of her wedding dress. The day was fine and some of the tension between them had eased. Once they were married, he was convinced the tension would cease entirely as they got to know each other under more normal circumstances.

The street in front of Hatchard's was busy and Beldon had to angle for a space to leave his tiger with the phaeton. He jumped down and went to assist Lilya. She stumbled on a rough piece of cobblestone when he set her down and he righted her. She laughed up at him, making light of her momentary clumsiness. This was the real Lilya, this beautiful, laughing woman.

For the moment her thoughts weren't filled with the diamond, weren't filled with fears for herself or for those around her. He would see to it that this woman emerged in her fullness. Not that he didn't also care for the Lilya who guarded the diamond. He did. He admired that woman, too; she was brave and courageous beyond measure. But that woman deserved peace. She deserved the right to lay down her burden and enjoy her life.

They had spent a delightful afternoon perusing the new books. Beldon had placed an order for the library at Pendennys, then it was time to meet Philippa at the dressmaker's.

He was boosting Lilya up into the high seat of the phaeton when it happened. A small boy, an urchin with grubby cheeks, ran up to him in the busy street. 'Are you Lord Pendennys? I have sumthin' for you.' He thrust a grimy sheet of paper at Beldon and tried to run away, but Beldon's reflexes were quicker. He held the boy by his collar.

'Who gave you this?' he demanded, scanning the perimeter of the street, well aware that Lilya was already standing up in the phaeton doing the same thing, a hand no doubt sliding towards her knife. His own view was limited by the position of the carriage and the busy traffic around him. For the first time, he felt his own vulnerability. In a press like this, he'd not see anyone coming until they were too close.

'I'm not to say. Lemme go.' The boy squirmed furiously beneath Beldon's hand.

'Let him go,' Lilya called, sitting down on the seat. 'Agyros didn't come himself. We'd never recognise the culprit.'

Beldon turned the boy loose and climbed up next to Lilya. 'What does it say?'

Lilya unfolded the paper and Beldon watched her hands tremble. She swallowed hard. Both of them had a good idea what the note would say. It would be a threat, of course. But knowing that didn't lessen the impact of reading the words scrawled on the page.

'May I see it?' Beldon asked tersely when she had enough time to digest the note. He gave the paper a rapid scan, his mouth taking on a grim line. 'The diamond in exchange for the safety of the family.'

Beldon saw the strategy at once. The note had been vague on purpose. In this case, the vague threat was the most potent. The note had not specified which family member, only that one family member would be taken in place of the diamond if she didn't turn the diamond over to Christoph Agyros by midnight tomorrow. It was rather bold of him to assume she had the diamond in her possession.

'It could be any one of you.' She fought the note of panic rising in her voice. 'What if…' her voice faltered '…what if Agyros has someone in Cornwall? What if they've taken Constantine or the baby?' Her nine-year-old brother and Valerian's one-year-old son had been left at the estate. They'd been deemed too young for a trip to London.

Beldon gripped her hands tightly. He felt her steady under his touch. He shook his head. 'It is doubtful. Agyros has no way to communicate with Cornwall. The estate is four days away and he's only given us a day to respond.

Lilya drew a deep breath. 'Then it's to be one of you,' she said quietly.

'I think he may find us less compliant than he expects. It would be rather hard to subdue Val or me.'

She turned wide eyes in his direction, his logic

raising a greater alarm. 'That's just it. Christoph and his henchmen, if he has any, have to know you and Val would put up a struggle, and quite possibly a struggle he and his men might lose. Which means it is not out of the realm of possibility that Christoph hasn't limited his use of the word "taken" to a mere kidnapping.'

Beldon chirped to his team and shook the reins, moving into traffic with grim determination. He wanted to reach the dressmaker's and Philippa with all due haste. That wedding dress needed to be done in record time.

Later, Lilya would not remember much of the afternoon, only that Beldon made all the arrangements and never left her side. Her world was a haze full of undefined images as the carriage drove her to the dressmaker and then home to Val's town house. Her own thoughts were consumed with what to do next. Either Val or Beldon was at risk and if she were to wager on it, she'd guess it was Beldon Christoph would come for.

Beldon was a whirlwind of plans by the time they reached the town house. Lilya let them plan. They had their own protection to think about now. She became aware that Beldon and Valerian were locked in heated debate.

'Val, you are to go with Philippa,' Beldon insisted. 'Just because Agyros can't pose a threat to the children in Cornwall tonight, doesn't mean he won't use the children later when he's had time to get into position.'

'You'll need me here,' Val protested.

'Your wife will need you there. Your duty is to your family,' Beldon argued fiercely.

Lilya saw a chance to protect them all. She raised her voice above the argument. 'You should go with them, Beldon.' It would be best this way. If they were safely off to protect her brother, she could slip out of the city and be gone. Beldon would only hear of her disappearance after it became too late to follow her. It would give him a way to honourably break the engagement. Surely he would see it was for the best.

Beldon was a study of disbelief. 'And what of you? I cannot leave you to face Agyros's machinations alone. Besides, we've discussed this before and you know my thoughts.'

It took all of Lilya's courage to face Beldon and say, 'I've managed to thwart him before this. I will continue to do so. My family's legacy demands it. Your place is with your family. The engagement ruse has not succeeded as we hoped. We must opt for Plan B.'

Beldon was not easily dismissed. His eyes flashed a stubborn challenge and it seemed to Lilya that a momentous decision had been reached somewhere in his head and he would not be swayed from it. 'Which is why we must be married with all haste in Cornwall. He will not dare to cross the wife of a peer. Write to him and tell him you do not have the diamond. When he hears of the wedding, perhaps he'll believe it.

'You do see this is your only chance? Lilya, you've worried so much about the rest of us, you haven't thought of yourself. He means to see you dead. If you don't have the diamond, you're expendable. If you do have the diamond, you'll live only long enough to give it to him. You'll barter it in the hope of saving one of us or yourself, but he will not honour any agreement.'

In her periphery, she saw Val and Philippa slip from the room, leaving them their privacy. She wondered just how much Beldon had told Val about their relationship.

'You are right to send Val with Philippa,' she said after they'd gone. 'But it's not him Christoph is after. It's you—Christoph means to use you against me.'

'I thought as much.' Beldon was all cool nonchalance, but his eyes burned with unmistakable desire.

She'd hoped her pronouncement would stun some reality into him. A man hunted him. A man wanted him dead because of his association with her. Surely that would put some modicum of fear into any rational being.

'Christoph is not fooling around. This is not an idle threat. Men have hunted the diamond across centuries. He has been sent by such people and he will not stop because one man stands in his way,' Lilya warned.

'Neither will I.' Beldon's hands were firm on her shoulders, warm and confident. 'I will not be thwarted because one man stands in my way.' He nipped gently at her ear lobe, his breath feathering erotically. 'I think Agyros will find I am not easy to kill. I wish you would believe me.' He knew her too well, he knew too well the path to the least of her resistance. His kisses were her weakness.

He tipped her head up, his mouth taking hers in a slow kiss. She sank into it, letting him trail kisses down her neck, revelling in the feel of his hand cupping the swell of her breast, his thumb teasing her nipple beneath the fabric. She moaned, thoroughly aroused by the boldness of his seduction, taking her to the fringe of the pleasure that awaited them if she dared—no, *when* she dared—to venture further.

Instinctively, her body knew something more lay beyond. These kisses, these caresses, were a mere prelude to something grander. He was promising it all to her if she'd only believe in him. Perhaps he understood that today, she needed to believe more than ever that he could keep the wolf of Christoph Agyros at bay through any means possible.

As if drawn there by some intuitive magnetism Lilya's hand slipped between them, seeking the source of his manly hardness. Finding it, she moulded its length beneath his trousers with slow wondrous strokes, exploring and pleasing as she went.

Beldon groaned, her name escaping his lips in a hoarse rasp of pleasure. 'Do you know what you do to me, Lilya?'

'You once said I made you smile.'

'Vixen,' he growled, taking her in a fierce kiss.

Lilya was giddy with the flood of life that coursed through her. Her body tingled, every nerve alive. She thought she might burst from the sheer thrill of it, standing with this man on the brink of the ultimate intimacy. With an intuition born of Eve, she knew exactly what she was about. Her decision was made. She did not want to wait for a wedding that was nothing more than a ruse. She wanted the raw passion that awaited her right now in this room, wanted to engage it and throw the darkness cast by Agyros aside, at least temporarily.

Chapter Twelve

Lilya took a step backwards so that Beldon could see all of her. The fire had burned down and only two lamps lit the room, bathing it in sensuous shadows of dusk. She raised one arm, slowly, deliberately, to the comb holding her coiffure in place, a half-smile lighting her lips, her eyes locked on his desire-darkened gaze. She pulled the comb in a single fluid motion, letting her hair spill down her back in a dark cascade. Her hands worked the laces at the back of her gown with incredible efficiency driven by her growing need for him.

Laces loose, she pushed the sleeves of her gown down her arms, the rest of her gown sliding to her feet in a puddle of silk until she stood before him, a tantalising offering, her body outlined through the thin linen of her undergarments by the room's dimming lights.

'Lilya, what are you doing?' Beldon's breath came hard, the question a rhetorical warning.

'I am seducing you, Beldon Stratten.' Never mind she didn't know precisely how to do that, but so far instinct had not betrayed her.

Beldon closed the gap between them. 'Let me finish. Raise your arms for me.' She did, letting him pull her chemise over her head. She divined his intentions immediately. With her arms raised, her breasts hung full and exposed, falling into his hands as if meant for them. He pressed her back to the sofa, laying her down. 'Let me look at you, Lilya,' he whispered.

And he looked. Oh, how he looked. She'd never been looked at in quite that way before, with his eyes, with his hands, and with his mouth, until Lilya thought she might die from the pleasure of it. The feel of his hands, of his mouth at her breasts, was exquisite, a pleasure undreamed of. It was more than the satisfying of a curiosity. This pleasure went straight to the core of her being and yet it was still not enough.

Beldon's hands moved to the waist of her pantalettes, slipping them over her hips, leaving her entirely uncovered to the air of the room. His hand was at the vulnerable intersection of her thighs. She arched against it in her impatience. 'Wait, Lilya, let me show you what your body needs.'

'It needs *you*.' Her voice was husky with want and rising desire. The life that had coursed through her earlier was a mere smoulder compared to the blaze Beldon had ignited now. She gave a throaty laugh. 'And here I'd thought to seduce you. It's turned out to be quite the other way around.'

'But you have seduced me, Lilya, oh, indeed you have, and quite thoroughly, too.' Beldon stood and quickly shed his shirt, his hands resting on the waist of his trousers. He drew a deep breath, as if fortifying himself. 'We can stop here.'

Lilya saw the effort such a statement cost him. 'No, we cannot.' She rose up from the sofa, propped on an elbow and reached for him, pulling him towards her. There was no turning back tonight. She wanted this man and tonight might be her only chance to claim him. She fumbled with the flap of his trousers and pushed them down over his lean hips, revelling in the sculpture of a man at his most private, most exposed. With her thumbs she traced the tapering muscles of his abdomen to the place where his hardness jutted upwards to greet her.

'I had no idea a man could be so beautiful,' she breathed, gently grasping him. 'Show me how to please you.'

He straddled her, giving her full access to him. 'Only for a short while. I want to last long enough to please us both.' Beldon's hand covered hers and moved it in a long stroke, down and back up.

He bucked beneath her hand and she revelled in the power of her ability to bring this man such gratification. Too soon, he halted her, shifting his body to cover her with the length of him. 'Your turn, now, our turn.' He kissed her fully on the mouth, his knee prodding her legs apart, his body settling between them. His hand was there, between her legs where she'd grown damp in her excitement and this time his hand caressed the intimate seam of her, surprising with a jolt of pleasure as his thumb found a hidden hub, a nucleus from which an extraordinary thrill radiated out to the rest of her body. She arched against him, her cry of delight silenced only by his kiss.

'Please,' she managed, her faculties slipping away in the wake of this new sensation.

He smiled down at her. 'I know,' he said simply. She felt the weight of his manhood at her entrance and then he was there, inside her, filling her. There was a jab of pain and her body tensed against the heretofore enjoyable invasion. Beldon stilled, withdrew and re-entered, this time without any impediment. She picked up his rhythm, her hips moving against his, urging him for more, desperate to reclaim the sensation that grew within her. Something cataclysmic loomed on the near horizon. Her body, her mind, reached for it, stretching towards it, driven there by the thrust of Beldon's body against hers.

Beldon was with her in this journey of ecstasy, his body leading hers, provoking hers to greater response until at last, he gave a mighty shudder that she felt at the very centre of her body, his strength and might pouring into her in an unquestionable act of claiming, of joining. She gave herself up to it entirely, knowing in the fibre of her being she was meant for this purpose, for this man, at least for a night, or maybe two, if fate was kind.

Beldon lifted a drowsy Lilya into his arms, a hall clock striking the late hour. She murmured a soft protest at being moved and nestled her head against his shoulder, lengths of her dark hair spilling over his arm. She looked like a princess from a fairy-tale book. His princess now. After what had transpired in the drawing room, there would be no turning back for either of them.

Beldon moved swiftly up the back stairs, careful to avoid any chance of running into Val or Philippa or any lingering late-night servants. He'd managed to decently drape Lilya in an elegant sofa throw, but nothing more. It was one thing if Val guessed what was occurring in the drawing room. It would be another to flaunt such behaviour in his face.

Of course, Beldon had not planned to fully seduce her in Val's drawing room. To his credit, he hadn't started it. But he'd certainly finished it, caught up in the madness of his own need and perhaps caught up in the intensity of Lilya's desperation, her desire to lose herself completely, to forget for a few moments about the diamond.

Even now when he thought himself thoroughly sated, he was hardening at the memory of her standing in the shadows of the fire, unveiling her body, her gown caressing her curves on its downwards spiral to the floor. Then she'd offered herself to him, every inch of that delectable body revealed and offered to him alone, the most incredible of gifts.

Beldon pushed open her bedroom door and deposited Lilya on the bed, arranging her blankets to keep her warm. He set aside her clothing and shoes and took a moment to study his sleeping bride. Taking her had not been part of his plan, but perhaps it should have been. If anything, tonight should have shown her that their marriage need not be a ruse. The passion between them held great promise for the future, a future that waited only for them to build it. He smoothed back a stray length of hair from her face. What had transpired between them had been extraordinary to him, far beyond the physically satisfying experiences he was used to with willing widows. He was still getting used to it, adjusting to it, processing it. A woman's pleasure had never meant so much to him as it had meant with Lilya.

He slipped from the room, wondering whether

perhaps, just perhaps, he was falling in love with his intended, which was something quite *unintended*.

In spite of his late night, Beldon was up early. There was much to do and he wanted to catch Valerian at breakfast before the house began the organised chaos of packing for the hasty journey back to Cornwall. True to form, Valerian was up when he arrived, breakfast set before him on a plate, coffee steaming at his right hand. A newspaper lay untouched beside him. But the signs of a difficult night were evident in the dark circles beneath his friend's eyes.

'She's yours now.' Valerian looked up from his food with a gaze that said he more than guessed what had passed in the night.

Beldon did not waver. 'She was mine the moment I put the announcement in *The Times*. I've never gone back on my word or needed an inducement to keep it. I will make her happy and I will make her safe.' Beldon helped himself to eggs and ham, scooping up a large spoonful of strawberries on the side.

'The marriage gambit may not work. Agyros may not be dissuaded,' Val mused out loud. 'Perhaps this risk is for naught.'

Beldon sat down with a shrug. 'It doesn't matter. Let him come. I am ready for him. I protect what is mine.'

He was aware of Val studying him for a long moment. 'But do you love her?'

Beldon gave a wry smile. 'Are you a poet now, Val? You've become quite the romantic.' He'd not anticipated falling in love with his wife, whoever she might have been when he'd laid his plans. 'I don't know about love at this point, Val.' When he'd begun his quest for a wife, he'd felt it best to limit his emotional offerings to respect and esteem, lest he become carried away as his father had been. 'But she has my admiration and my support. I think, too, that she is not indifferent to me.'

It was Val's turn to shrug. 'Love is one of life's great pleasures and not to be missed. I wish it for both your sakes. Love can change a man, for the better; make him appreciate what truly matters in this one life.'

'Well, think of it this way, everything is working out just as we'd planned when we were young.' Beldon offered Val a consoling smile.

Val nodded, both of them remembering the day the two of them and Philippa had pledged to be together always. It was the day before he and Val had left for school, the first term after Val's parents had died and emotions were running high. Philippa had been twelve, they'd been a grown-up fifteen. Back then, no one would have guessed Val would end up married to Philippa. But here they all were: Philippa and Val parents, Val's estate restored, Beldon's home finally out of debt and ready for its mistress.

Val broke the silence. 'Don't misunderstand, I'm delighted, of course. I could not wish for Lilya a finer man and you are my best friend, even if I wish the circumstances were different.'

'We will not let those circumstances cloud the joy of a wedding.' Philippa swept into the room, stopping to plant a kiss on Val's cheek. 'By the time you and Lilya arrive in Cornwall, we'll have all the details set. You only have to decide if you want to marry at Pendennys or at St Justus.'

'Pendennys, I think,' Beldon said without equivocation, 'in the little stone chapel where our parents married.'

'It will be lovely. Everyone deserves a beautiful wedding, no matter what the cause. Lilya's dress will be done at the end of the week and then it's up to you when you want to come down,' Philippa advised warily, worry evident in the furrow of her brow. Beldon read her thoughts easily. The blackmail deadline was tonight at midnight and no one truly knew what that deadline would bring.

Noon brought the St Just travelling coach, ready for departure, to the front of the town house. Travelling trunks were strapped on top and behind. Philippa had worked a miracle with packing and leaving instructions for the staff, while Valerian briefed Beldon on who to contact if he needed help, most of which Beldon knew already. But he could see it eased Valerian's anxiety over leaving.

Valerian's plain-clothed hired men would remain outside the town house as long as Lilya was in residence. Beldon would stay on here as well. For Lilya's protection, he would not return to Pendennys House. He'd sent a set of his own instructions on ahead to close up Pendennys House and to prepare for a removal to Cornwall much earlier than expected. He'd also sent for his own personals and clothes to be brought over.

No one spoke of diamonds or blackmail as Beldon and Lilya stood on the steps of the town house to wave off the carriage. Philippa hugged Beldon. 'Are you sure you won't come? Both of you? Perhaps coming to Cornwall with us will be safer after all? Safety in numbers?' Worry was evident in her eyes.

'Do not worry. We shall handle everything here,' Beldon reassured her. He and Valerian had decided sending Lilya to Cornwall with them would quite likely invite an attack on the road where they'd be unable to protect themselves. The risk was unacceptable.

'We'll follow later. You'll see us soon.' Beldon kissed his sister's cheek. 'That's for my nephew when you see him.' He did mean to spirit Lilya out of town, but it must be done covertly and under the cover of night. Theirs would be an escape. Even though they'd made it public knowledge the wedding would be in Cornwall, Beldon preferred to travel as secretly as possible. An unpersuaded Agyros could make mischief on the road for them.

Valerian helped Philippa into the carriage and shut the door behind him. The carriage pulled away from the curb and Beldon felt Lilya slip her hand into his. Beldon made a show of waving to the coach. If the house were being watched, Christoph would know the viscount and his wife had departed. They'd departed well before the midnight deadline, putting them effectively out of reach. Even if Christoph had not planned on coming after Beldon, he had no choice now with Val and Philippa gone. If he meant to enforce his threat, he had to go through Beldon.

Beldon turned into the house, ushering Lilya before him. Grim determination settled on his shoulders. His friend and sister were off to safety. He'd drawn the attentions of the man who'd threatened his soon-to-be wife to himself. He would have it no other way. All those he cared about were protected to the best of his abilities for the moment.

The moment the door shut behind them, Lilya bolted for the back parlour. Facing Beldon the morning after—or rather the afternoon after—was far more difficult than she had imagined. She'd awakened to find herself in her bed, stark naked beneath the blankets, with a very clear recollection of how she'd come to be in such a state.

The good news was that she was no longer focused on his lips when he was in the room. The bad news was that she was now focused on other unmentionable male parts. It begged the question: would she always look at him and picture him gloriously naked from now on? She had yet to look at him today without mentally erasing his clothes. She was not immune to the consequences of her imaginings. She was fast learning that every action had its own reciprocal. Her body recalled with acute accuracy how a naked Beldon made it feel.

Lilya chose a book at random from the glass-fronted case in the little room, determined to lose herself in whatever she'd chosen—a history, a treatise, perhaps. She settled on the sofa, legs curled beneath her and opened the book.

Damn and double damn.

Sonnets.

Love sonnets.

Maybe it was a sign she shouldn't be looking for distraction. She was distracted enough. Just when she needed all her wits to outmanoeuvre Christoph, they seemed to have left her altogether. If she'd been the Lilya who'd first come to England, she would have fled in the night without hesitation. That girl was gone. In her place was a woman who was tired of running, who wanted to stand and fight in the hopes that she might win, no matter that the odds indicated her chances were minimal.

When that had changed for her, she couldn't say. But it had definitely changed. Perhaps the change had begun with Val and Philippa. Life in the peace of their household had been a potent lure. Normalcy was an enticing luxury.Perhaps it had been Beldon's hot kisses, the explosive way he made her feel when she was in his arms, as if they could conquer the world. That didn't mean she wouldn't run ever again. If running was the only way to protect those around her, she would do it. It just meant she'd rather stay. If she could.

Most unfortunately, along with capitulating to marriage, she'd also managed to fall in love. Lilya traced an idle pattern on the sofa with her finger. How had it come to this? She'd been so careful to guard against falling in love. She'd promised herself she'd never endanger people she cared for as her father had. It had been easy to promise such things to herself when she hadn't truly understood the price. When she'd made these pledges she had not dreamed the cost would be so high.

The costs weren't just about the diamond, although those were plenty. She was a woman in love with a man who didn't love her, and that posed a dangerous set of questions. Would Beldon have ever offered for her if not for the diamond? Would he ever have fallen for Lilya Stefanov if she hadn't been a damsel in distress? She didn't know because she barely knew who she was without the diamond. Who was she if she wasn't the secret-keeper of *Adamao*?

'I thought I'd find you here.' Beldon lounged in the doorway, conjured from her very thoughts, the very epitome of masculinity, coatless and rolled-up shirt sleeves. Something primal flickered in his eyes. For a moment she thought he was going to devour her on the sofa and her stomach flipped over in anticipation. Then the fires in his eyes banked. He held out his hand and said, 'It's time to write the letter.'

Lilya's heart sank.

Ah, yes. The diamond. The damned diamond. When Beldon looked at her, he saw the diamond for different reasons than Christoph Agyros, but he still saw the diamond. She wished he didn't.

Chapter Thirteen

Dear Mr Agyros,

I regret to inform you that your request that a
certain gem be put into your care has met with
disapproval and confusion. I believe you have mistaken me for someone else, perhaps. I am not in
possession of said item. Nor do I approve of being
approached in such a threatening manner.

I must politely request that you do not attempt
to seek me out any further. Your pursuit of me is
unseemly. As I am sure you are aware, I am about
to marry and must terminate contact with you out
of respect for my future husband.

Lilya Stefanov

Christoph crumpled the note in his hand. She regretted to inform him? She'd regret it soon enough and

But his resolve did nothing to appease Lilya.

'Midnight has come and gone. Agyros knows he does not have the diamond. He's had time now to ponder what he'll do next. He has only two choices; do something or do nothing. If he chooses the latter, his blackmail is a sham without influence.'

Something was definitely wrong. His nonchalance did not fool her. Beldon was different this morning. Lilya could see it. There was grimness to his features, his eyes hard and alert, his body tense.

Someone looking at him in passing would not know it. His *toilette* was immaculate, his clothes crisp and pressed, his jaw smoothly shaven. But further study revealed the tiny chinks in his gentlemanly armour. He chatted pleasantly with her during the drive and for once his attentions were not focused on her. Those blue eyes of his periodically and methodically darted into the crowds around them on the street, especially when they came to a full stop, as they were now. A large dray was unloading in front of a shop and progress around it was slow.

There were other tell-tale signs of unease. He'd opted to take Philippa's town landau when he could have driven Valerian's curricle or his own phaeton and taken the ribbons himself, a task she knew Beldon enjoyed. He seldom had himself driven anywhere. He was too much of a horseman to deny himself the pleasure. The other concerning feature was the presence of his walking stick, a sleek affair of cherry wood and polished brass. Val had a sword-stick inside his. She'd wager a monkey Beldon did, too. She was no idiot. In spite of the seemingly harmless trip to the dressmaker's, Beldon was anticipating trouble, welcoming it even.

The carriage inched forwards and Lilya decided to tackle the issue. 'What do you expect to happen, Beldon? It's clear you expect something so it's no use trying to lie.'

His answer was cryptic. 'I simply want to be prepared. We cannot stay boxed up at home for ever, but neither can we ignore the dangers when we do go out.' At least he hadn't tried to deny it. Perhaps his preparations were simply precautions after all. Well, she could be prepared, too.

She'd taken to quartering the street with her gaze these past few blocks, but riding backwards, Beldon had the advantage. He could see behind them. She could only see ahead of them. Someone *following* the landau wouldn't want to get ahead of them. Out of a reflexive need for comfort, she felt for her knife. Today, it rode low on her leg, strapped to her calf so she only had to flick her skirts to reach it. A knife high on her thigh wouldn't be easily accessible in public.

If there was an attack, when would it come? Would it come while they were trapped in traffic? The thought made Lilya uneasy. 'Perhaps we should get out and walk,' she suggested.

'We're nearly there. The shop is just the next street up once we get past the dray.'

But we're sitting ducks, Lilya wanted to protest. Maybe that's what Beldon intended. Did he want to draw Christoph's attentions? They had no idea how Christoph meant to come after them—a gun, a knife, a kidnapping and torment? She shuddered to think of it. The *Filiki Adamao* was ruthless and she did not know how she'd endure it if Beldon were tortured. To watch him be slowly murdered, knowing she could stop it if she turned over the jewel, was something she didn't want to contemplate. If they were taken, there'd be no real hope of escape except death. They'd be killed regardless of what she gave up. In the end it would only be a matter of mercy. That's how the *Filiki* operated.

The crowds parted and for an instant Lilya caught sight of a man staring in their direction. She reached for Beldon's hand. 'There, over to the left, can you see him? He's staring at us.'

Beldon turned his head to look, but was distracted. 'Money, for a poor veteran, good sir?' A vagrant approached the other side of the landau, apparently taking advantage of the stalled traffic.

'There he is!' Lilya gave a hushed cry and tugged at Beldon's sleeve. He glanced over his shoulder. The crowd shifted and they saw the danger together. The man had moved into position slightly ahead of the carriage, a pistol raised hastily and his target clear.

Beldon reacted first, roughly shoving her to the floor of the carriage, but not before the man got off a shot. She felt rather than saw Beldon lunge to the far side of the carriage. Foolish man! Didn't he understand the bullet was meant for him? Not her. No one dared to shoot her, not yet, not while she alone possessed the diamond.

There were other screams now, people running to get out of the way of the nameless terror. The street was alive with panic, horses and people caught up in the noisy aftermath of the shot. Lilya could feel the carriage rock as people raced past, bumping the vehicle in their haste to get away. From the sound of things, the driver was struggling with the spooked horses.

Where was Beldon? She'd felt his weight against one side of the carriage, but that weight was gone now. He was no longer in the landau with her.

Gathering her courage, Lilya rose up from the floor, slipping out her knife from beneath her skirt. What she saw horrified her. In the midst of the stampeding crowd surging around the carriage, two men grappled with Beldon and the coachman for control of the vehicle by pulling them off the bench. Lilya recognised the assailants immediately: the vagrant and the man with the gun. The coachman struck out valiantly with his long whip, but it was minimally effective in close fighting. Beldon parried blows with his swordstick.

That was when she noticed something was wrong. Beldon wielded the stick with his left hand as opposed to his usual right. Beldon struggled, losing his balance momentarily. Lilya's breath caught, her eyes drawn to the crimson stain at Beldon's shoulder. The bullet had found its target after all.

Beldon pushed back his attacker with a well-placed boot to the stomach. He regained his feet in a rolling lurch, signs of pain evident in his stance. She had to do something! If they pulled Beldon down, Christoph would have the leverage he needed to negotiate. If they took him, how could she not trade the diamond for his release?

Lilya hefted the small, perfectly balanced knife in her hand. No one paid her any attention. Beldon and the coachman's backs were to her, their bulk blocking her from the attention of the two assailants.

Beldon's attacker regrouped from being kicked in the stomach and charged again. This time Lilya didn't wait. She rose up, exposing her presence for the moment and threw the knife, hitting Beldon's attacker squarely and effectively in the shoulder.

The would-be assailant screamed in shocked pain, his eyes looking beyond Beldon for the source of his agony. 'The bitch stabbed me!'

Beldon snarled, and with a shove sent him sprawling backwards into the street in final defeat. It was enough to turn the engagement their way. Seeing his accomplice wounded and useless, the other man quickly retreated into the mob and disappeared. Beldon fell back on to the bench seat, clutching his shoulder and breathing hard.

'Drive! Drive!' Lilya shouted the moment they were free.

Grabbing up the fallen reins, the coachman leapt to action, forcing a path through the scattering crowd, the sudden movement throwing Lilya back into her seat. Her mind was racing, her heart was racing in the aftermath.

Fear came to Lilya for the first time since she'd spotted the man in the crowd. Her warning had come too late. For all his courage, Beldon was not immortal, a fact attested to by the crimson stain rapidly spreading across his back. The bullet had entered the shoulder from behind. She wanted Beldon to come sit with her, she wanted to see the extent of the injury, but he made no move to join her as the carriage bowled along the streets home to the St Just house. Dear Lord, there was a lot of blood. Beldon had his hand over his shoulder, but she could see his hand was red in an attempt to staunch the wound.

Had the shot been intended for his shoulder or had his quick turn at her cry ruined the intended target? If he had not moved, the bullet could easily have found its way to his head. Lilya shuddered against the gruesome contemplations. She grabbed up her shawl from the seat beside her. 'Here, Beldon, use this.' She handed him the shawl. He took it with his left hand, his face pale and grim in profile. He said nothing.

'Please, let it be better than it looks,' Lilya murmured.

In her mind, she went over all that would need doing when they arrived home. She would have to call for Val's physician and there would be a surgery to set up. At the least, Beldon's shoulder would need stitching. At the worst, the bullet was still lodged inside.

At the town house, Lilya jumped down from the carriage, shouting orders. 'Get the baron in the house, draw the curtains. Someone go for the viscount's doctor. The baron's been shot.' Val's men were well trained and every one leapt into action. Footmen mobilised with alacrity to set up a surgery in the drawing room. It was all handled with such ease, Lilya had to wonder just how much experience they'd had with such things.

Beldon reluctantly let a footman help him down from the driver's bench, trying desperately to not need assistance, but Lilya could see the effort his bravado cost him in the paleness of his face and the sweat on his brow. 'There's no need to be stubborn,' she said, walking close to Beldon's other side.

'There's every need,' he ground out between gritted teeth, making the slow walk up Val's front steps.

'We want Christoph to think it was only a minor scratch.'

Oh, no. Did that mean it wasn't? Lilya's stomach plummeted. Was it more than blood and pain?

His next words confirmed it, his left hand reaching out to grasp hers for a moment as they stepped inside. 'Lilya, I can't feel my arm.'

Beldon's concentration amazed her. It would have been easy to give in to blessed unconsciousness throughout his ordeal with the doctor. But Beldon struggled to remain alert, a feat of physical and mental fortitude. If he could be stubborn, she could be, too.

The housekeeper urged her to lie down and rest. They would let her know how it all went after the doctor's visit. But Lilya would not be dislodged from Beldon's side. He was her responsibility. She had caused this.

The bullet was still lodged in a tricky part of the shoulder. It would need to come out. That was all Lilya needed to know to roll up her sleeves.

Lilya laboured by the doctor through the long process of removing the bullet, fighting her squeamishness valiantly. She'd worked in a war zone before, but it was far different when the warrior was the man you loved. Lilya felt each painful probe as if it were her own flesh.

'There it is, I can feel it,' the doctor said with the

satisfaction of a small victory. Moments later the doctor held up a tiny ball of steel before plunking it into a small dish. 'Fortunately for him the ball didn't shatter,' the doctor declared triumphantly, reaching for a needle. 'I'll close the wound and we'll be finished.'

'Will he be all right now?' Lilya was desperate for good news even though she knew they weren't out of the woods yet.

The doctor looked at her dubiously. 'If he can avoid infection.'

'And his arm? Can he feel it?' Lilya pressed.

The doctor shrugged, pausing in mid-stitch. 'Hard to say. It might have been the bullet's pressure on some nerves that caused the numbness. With the bullet gone, feeling will gradually return. But...' he held up his hand in warning '...the bullet may have ruined some nerves and severed the connection altogether.'

'When can he be moved?'

'Upstairs?' the doctor questioned, tying off his stitches.

'No, to Cornwall.' She had to get Beldon home. If Christoph knew Beldon was indisposed, he might become more aggressive.

'Oh, my dear, he shouldn't attempt to travel for a month; perhaps a couple of weeks if it was an emergency and it was handled with the utmost care. Aside from the injury to his arm, he did lose blood.'

A month? Two weeks? Impossible. She had a day or two.

The doctor placed a kindly hand on her shoulder. 'Be thankful, my dear, that the baron has come through this relatively well. But I wouldn't want to push luck any further. Give him time.'

Lilya watched the doctor go. Time was the one thing she couldn't give Beldon. She sighed and leaned her head against the wall. She would stay until he was out of danger and then...well, and then she'd do what she should have done from the start before she'd begun to believe things could be different. She would leave and the danger would leave with her. After the scandal passed, he could go on to marry Lady Eleanor and she, well, she'd just go on. Surely, Beldon would agree the brief scandal of a broken engagement was an affordable price to pay for a life, especially when the life was his.

Chapter Fourteen

'Tell me everything—what did the doctor say?' Beldon was awake and irritable, with understandable reason, of course.

'You should be asleep,' Lilya countered with a smile. When she'd slipped out of the room to speak with the doctor, she'd thought he'd finally drifted off. She went to the sofa and knelt beside him, smoothing back his hair from his forehead. 'You're safe now, you don't have to be brave or stubborn. I know you must be tired and you must be in pain. I have laudanum the doctor left.'

'No.' Beldon was surprisingly adamant. If it had been her, she didn't know if she'd be able to resist the temporary promise of relief.

'Rest will help you heal faster.'

Beldon tried to push himself up into a sitting position with one good arm. 'Rest will see us dead.'

Noting his struggle, Lilya snatched up a little pillow from a nearby chair and settled it behind him. 'We'll be fine. No one will get past Val's men.'

'And perhaps we'll never get out.' Beldon's tone was grim.

Lilya swallowed. 'We'll find a way.' What could she say to that? If Christoph could hire men willing to fire at Beldon in a crowd, what else would they be willing to do? To Beldon? To her?

Thankfully, Beldon's eyes began to shut. Rest was determined to find him no matter how much he resisted. Lilya watched his face smooth into sleep. She was tired, too, now that the initial dangers had faded, but she had to think.

Beldon was right. Staying barricaded in Valerian's town house was a stalemate at best, no substitute for victory. Victory here was all she could tolerate. There was no negotiation possible and defeat was unthinkable.

But tempting.

She'd known all along that her life could never include Beldon and the diamond in spite of the moments when she'd tried to fool herself. It would always be Beldon *or* the diamond. Maybe she should give it up, simply stuff it into an envelope and send it by courier to Christoph.

She would be free. Maybe. Maybe he'd see her

dead anyway now that she had too much knowledge and no more usefulness.

Impossible.

Give up the diamond.

Give up her family's deadly legacy.

The argument for doing so was powerful. Her family was shattered. She had only young Constantine left. Her life was here in England now. She did not owe the Phanariot community anything, felt no particular loyalty to it. Her legacy had seen her covertly chased from its circles. Whatever loyalty she felt was to her father and the promise she'd given him.

Then she'd have to live with the guilt. She'd still have a legacy, only it would have transmuted from a diamond to guilt, to cowardice. A woman had her pride as much as a man did. Lilya's word meant something to her. She could see the looming complications of this choice. The diamond would still be between her and Beldon even if it wasn't physically present.

She would come to hate herself for her betrayal and that would sour their love. They would both spend their lives living with the knowledge that she'd given up the diamond in exchange for him. For her it would mean guilt, and for Beldon it would mean doubt—did she ever regret her choice? Did he live up to her expectations, had he been worth the price?

Mere ripples on the pond. The consequences

didn't stop there. Lilya reached out to adjust the blanket covering Beldon, twitching it to her satisfaction. It was selfish to think only of herself and Beldon in this decision. Giving up the diamond wasn't just about her life. It was about the lives of unseen thousands.

The people who hunted the diamond were not pure of intentions. No one who used the methods subscribed to by Christoph Agyros acted in good faith. The people who wanted the diamond had covert and nefarious intentions for the gem. With the independence of Greece at hand, the Balkans would realign again into different boundaries and alliances. There would be room for upheaval, for people to seize power. It had been the first thing she'd thought of last year when news had reached her of the assassination of Ioannis Kapodistrias. There were those among the Phanariots who did not want Greece to achieve independence.

In an independent Greece the Phanariots would no longer be princes of the Danubian provinces, would no longer hold a position of power within the Ottoman Empire. Instead, independence would bring an abrupt reversal of their social status. Phanariots would go from being wealthy and privileged members of society to being a suspect and traitorous people. Her people, cast down, princes no more.

The diamond could change that while everything

hung in the balance and much remained undecided. The diamond could finance an army. In the hands of the right people, it could sustain Phanariot power and prevent independence or it could control whatever king sat on the newly created throne. Either way, it would preserve Phanariot power even as it corrupted true independence—independence her father had fought and died for years earlier.

The temptation to find personal victory in the defeat of turning over the diamond to Christoph Agyros receded. She could not do it. In these dark moments, Lilya longed for her father and his wisdom. Had her father ever been tempted like this? Had he ever wanted to simply lay down the burden? Had he ever weighed the small lives of his family against the lives of soldiers and nations?

The father she remembered had always seemed so sure of his convictions, of his direction. Growing up, he'd taught them all to hold fast in the face of adversity. The man who stood for nothing, but changed courses with every wind, would fall at the slightest provocation. Had she been wrong in assuming it had been an easy course for him?

Lilya slumped in her chair, filled with a strange feeling of relief. She'd passed the test. But there'd be more to come. She'd wounded the man today who'd shot at Beldon. Christoph would be furious. But perhaps it would slow him down if he needed to hire a replacement. Perhaps she had a day or two to see to Beldon and get him through the risk of infection. And then what? Then it would be time to leave. Alone.

Beldon awoke with a start, his mind consumed with one thought: Lilya. He had to protect Lilya. There was a man with a gun. He jerked and groaned with the pain of true remembrance. He'd been shot. Flashes came to him: the suddenness of the attack, of throwing Lilya beneath him to safety before he climbed on to the box to help the driver; of Lilya throwing her knife with deadly accuracy to thwart his attacker; of Lilya pale-faced and stoic, helping the doctor. There'd been worry in her face. That at least was reassuring. She cared for him at least a little. That was an admirable quality in one's wife. She more than cared, he knew that. Her desire for him was real. That kind of passion could not be faked. But she would deny that desire for the sake of her legacy. Time was of the essence on several fronts. He supposed he was lucky she was still here.

How long had he slept? Long shadows mixed with light peeped around the edges of the curtains. It wasn't early morning, nor was it night. His shoulder throbbed, his arm was tingling uncomfortably. That particular pain was a good sign. He recalled he hadn't been able to feel it before, it had been entirely numb. He couldn't move without the support of his shoulder and he desperately wanted to get up and attend to some suddenly very insistent needs.

His eyes adjusted to the room and he could make out a figure in one of Val's wing-backed chairs. Lilya. Her presence brought a quick smile to his lips. But he'd be damned if he was going to ask her to bring him a chamber pot like an invalid. A man had his pride and his was already wounded from the outing today.

He'd failed her. His plan to expose Agyros's next move had certainly succeeded, but not as he'd expected. He'd not thought they'd be foolish enough or daring enough, depending on how one looked at it, to fire a shot in broad daylight. He'd expected fists and knives in an alley. He'd been ready for that. He'd had no chance of defending himself against a random shot. Only Lilya's warning had caused him to turn. A shoulder wound was far less than what had been intended. If Lilya had not seen the man, Beldon knew he would be dead.

He knew, too, that if Lilya hadn't thrown her knife when she did the fight might have gone a different direction. Instead of forcing off the attackers, they might have been overcome and held for the ransom of the diamond. It was a bitter pill to swallow to know that, for all his protestations of protection, Lilya had been the one to ultimately save the day. Dressed up in satins and silks, one easily forgot the slender beauty possessed an iron core forged from resolve and experience—a veritable Boadicea in lace, was his Lilya.

His bladder protested. It looked as if he'd have to swallow another proverbial pill. 'Lilya,' he called out hoarsely.

She stirred and stretched. 'You're awake. How do you feel? I'll get you some water.'

Definitely no on the water. 'Perhaps you could call me a footman first?'

She looked perplexed by the request. *Please don't make me say it*, Beldon groaned inwardly. It would embarrass them both. The intimacy of making love was one thing. This was another and he wasn't ready for it. 'I'll just need a minute and then we can talk.'

'Of course,' Lilya assented, perhaps divining his meaning, and hurried out of the room, or perhaps just catering to an injured man's whims.

It took two footmen to help him rise. All of his effort was concentrated on battling the overwhelming dizziness. Logically, he knew it to be from blood loss, but the knowledge didn't help steady his reeling world. His mind was whirling in other ways, too. There were plans to make. There was Lilya to protect. The least he could do was try again in that regard. If he knew Lilya, she was already planning to run. She would see today's attack as proof that nothing could stop the *Filiki Adamao*.

Settled once more on the sofa against steadying pillows and blessedly upright, Beldon waited for

male who must face the enemy alone. You're not the only one who can protect. It's not fair to protect me and not extend the same privilege to me. Men aren't the only ones who protect those they love.' She paused here, the loudest part of her anger spent, replaced by something else. Sadness, perhaps?

He was touched by her intentions. 'Lilya, you did protect me today. You were the one who called the warning, you were the one who stabbed our villain. Without you, I would be dead.'

'No, you'd be alive. Alive and unharmed, dancing attendance on Lady Eleanor Braithmore as you intended. Don't you see, Beldon? It's too dangerous to be with me. I've done nothing but upset your carefully ordered life. I do not want another man to put himself between me and a bullet again.'

Beldon grumbled, 'You make it sound like that's a recurring theme.'

'It is,' she said sharply. Then something crumpled in her face, all the fire subdued, replaced by a certain sadness. 'There was a boy in Constantinople when I was sixteen.'

'A boy you liked?' Beldon ventured.

Lilya nodded. 'Benjamin. He was seventeen and he thought…' She paused here, overcome with emotion. Her eyes misted over, going back in time, seeing things that were not in this room. She shook her head. 'Suffice it to say, he thought many of the same things you thought and he died.'

'And that's when you decided you would not fall in love again.' He was starting to see the reasons for her resistance to marriage more clearly now. He could understand her choice to remain alone. She was afraid to love, afraid of the pain that would inevitably come. They weren't so very different in that regard.

'I'd already decided that. My father's love for his family destroyed it,' Lilya said sharply, gathering up the tray. No, they weren't so very different at all. He understood the well-meant sins of a father all too well.

'Put the tray down, Lilya. It will keep. I want you to send for the carriage and have a few essentials packed. Clothes, blankets, bandages, a hamper of food. As soon as everything is ready, tell the servants they may have a few days off duty. I don't want them around if Christoph comes calling.' His head was settling, the world was slowing to its correct pace.

'Trust me, everything will be all right. Now, go pack your things, and I'll give a footman instructions about what to pack for me. But come back when you're done.'

Chapter Fifteen

Lilya surveyed the carriage neatly parked in the mews, mentally reviewing all she had packed. There was a large hamper of food under the seat, blankets stacked on the other with a basket of medical supplies, a travelling trunk strapped to the back. Everything was neat and organised. It was not the panicked mish-mash of an escape. Lilya felt in her pocket for the diamond, the one thing she had not trusted to a trunk or travelling case.

She needed the diamond on her person at all times now. No longer could she live with the luxury of knowing it was safely tucked away in a hat box or beneath a floorboard. Just as she remembered fondly that first day, she bitterly rued the day Christoph Agyros introduced himself in the park. That day marked the beginning of her troubles, the day that led to this day when she'd had to 'put on' the diamond again. Slipping it into her secret pocket beneath her skirt had been akin to taking on a weight or a shackle, but there was nothing to be done about that now.

Beldon waited inside and there were still instructions to give the staff. Beldon's carriage was as ready as she could make it. All that remained out here was the harnessing of the horses. The coachman would do that at dusk so all would be ready. The horses might have to stand a bit before it was fully dark enough to depart, but Lilya wanted to leave nothing to chance.

Lilya drew a deep breath and squared her shoulders. She had to go back in and see to phase two of their discreet evacuation.

Inside, orders had been followed with precision. Val's staff understood implicitly the reasons behind the requests and went errorlessly about their jobs. Lilya stopped to talk with the housekeeper. 'The upstairs maids have been sent home?'

'Yes, miss, the maids have all been sent home. It's just the footmen here now. They're taking the valuables up to the attics. If anyone comes to the house, they'll find very little to take with them unless they want to carry a chair down the street.'

Lilya smiled. 'You've done splendidly, then, and in such a short time.' Lilya hoped their efforts would be enough. She didn't think Christoph would burn the place. But he would not leave anything unturned if he thought the diamond was still here or if he was angry enough to want revenge. He would not like knowing she had slipped past him again.

Beldon looked up as she entered the drawing room. He had a shirt on, which must have been no small feat even with help, and his arm rested in sling. 'How are things going out there? It doesn't seem nearly as chaotic as it ought to be,' he joked. Lilya took it as a good sign. The hoarseness had faded from his voice and his blue eyes were still clear. No fever yet. Hopefully no fever ever, although she fully expected there would be. She just hoped it wouldn't be bad. Some fever she could deal with on the road, but a raging fever would be difficult.

'It's time to go.' Two footmen came and helped him to the carriage. It was the last thing to do. Lilya climbed in once he was settled and shut the door, giving permission for the coach to set off.

'You've dismissed the staff?' Beldon asked, a bit winded from the exertions of the move. Beads of sweat stood out on his brow and she hoped they were from the exertions, too.

'They're just putting the last of the valuables away,' she assured him.

'I had not thought of that,' Beldon said with admiration. 'You're good at this sort of thing.'

'*Hospodars* have some practice at "this sort of thing",' she said lightly. They'd only gone a few streets and she could see the effort it cost him to travel, the constant rocking of the coach jostling his arm.

He managed a wry smile, acknowledging that she saw his pain. 'Distract me, Lilya. Come sit beside me and tell me why is that you're good at this sort of thing?'

She obliged, moving to his side of the carriage and taking his good hand in her own, as happy to have something to do as he had of distraction. 'Well,' she began, 'the life of a *hospodar* is inherently dangerous. As a tax collector to the sultan, the serfs beneath you don't always admire your status. You are someone to be trusted warily. You may overcharge people. And, of course, even though people don't trust you, they want to be your friend since you have the power to grant favours. So, in return, you can't really trust anyone yourself. Everyone's using everyone. Then there's the sultan, who is always and perhaps rightfully paranoid.'

'It's the sultan's own fault. He should not have set up a system where he is so reliant on a group of people for his own interactions with the rest of the world,' Beldon argued. 'This is a paranoia of his own making.'

'Oh, indeed it is,' Lilya readily agreed. She took it as a good sign that he was alert enough to follow her story. 'Years ago, the sultans looked to the Phanariots to act as go-betweens. The empire forbade the speaking of any language other than Arabic, the holy language of the Koran. This made communicating with the French, the Russians, the British, impossible without the Phanariots. It was one of the reasons our power had grown so large. The sultan appointed us to vital positions in the government until the Phanariots were responsible for the majority of the empire's foreign policy.

'With dire consequences,' Lilya continued, idly tracing the lines of Beldon's hand. 'Many of the *hospodars* were double-dealing. Without the ability to communicate in other languages, the sultan had people plotting revolutions beneath his nose.' She paused. 'Like my father. In the end, he could not balance himself between multiple loyalties any longer: loyalty to his belief in independence and the need for a separate Christian state; loyalty to the wealth of the sultan, which provided so magnificently for his family; and his loyalty to the Phanariot community. He'd given his word to protect it from the diamond.' Lilya sighed. 'This… Beldon? Are you awake?' She laughed softly in the darkness. Somewhere during her dissertation, he'd fallen asleep. She pressed a hand to his forehead and breathed relief. No fever yet.

Lilya fell quiet, her ears straining for anything untoward on the road. They were far outside London now. The race for Cornwall had officially begun if anyone discovered their absence and dared to pursue. It was better to think of that than to think of what lay at the end of the road: a wedding to a man she had fallen in love with whether he loved her or not. She hoped that the wedding was not a prelude to his funeral or, worse, that she'd live to regret the decision.

Christoph Agyros sliced a sofa pillow in abject frustration. Everyone had gone. Even the servants. The cunning little witch had escaped and who knew how long ago? Had she left an hour ago? Two hours? How had she managed it with a wounded man? He'd meant to come alone in the night when the servants were asleep and it was just her and the wounded baron. He'd felt sure Lilya, in her panic, would have been ready to bargain for lives with the diamond. But she hadn't panicked. She'd managed to pack a wounded man off and leave the city hours before he'd arrived. Not even her departure had the signs of chaos. The silver had been locked up and the servants dismissed—the latter done on purpose, no doubt. Their absence served to protect Lilya's destination. Not that it was a secret. Lilya and Pendennys had gone to Cornwall to celebrate their wedding, fabricated or no, and to be safe.

Christoph growled. The last thing he wanted was to make a gruelling journey all the way to Roseland–St Just, especially when she would be on the alert for him. He let himself out of the town house by the alley gate. He would give Lilya this small victory as a wedding gift. She could have her getaway. She could even have her wedding and a little honeymoon. He had business in town with the talks progressing. Prince Otto was going to be given the Greek throne and borders were being decided. It would be important to be the *Filiki*'s eyes and ears for those discussions. Once that was done, he'd go to Cornwall and surprise Lilya out of her new-found complacency when she was least expecting it, when she thought she could have peace at last.

There was no place he'd rather be, Beldon thought, raising the shade to let the late-morning sun come through. They were on the long road from Roseland—St Just to Pendennys, the homeward road. Across from him, Lilya slept the sleep of the truly exhausted, finally worn out from four days of vigilance. Violet smudges populated the space beneath her eyes. When she awoke, they'd be home. Outside, the twilight world was green, wildflowers growing up by the sides of the road. He was home thanks to luck and Lilya.

They'd managed to elude any discovery for four days. They'd stopped at inns in the evenings. He'd kept his hat low and always taken off his sling when in public and Lilya had kept the hood of her cloak drawn close about her face.

So far luck had served them on all accounts. They had not been pursued. His wound had not festered,

nor given him much of a fever after the first day,
although it had hurt like the dickens from all the
jouncing over the road. Even his fine carriage could
not save him from all the ruts, but he could stand a
little pain. Best of all, the feeling had returned to his
arm and his worries of permanent damage could be
laid to rest. It could always be worse, as his grand-
mother had been fond of saying. Indeed, in this case
it could have been far worse than it had been.

Lilya stirred, the travelling rug about her drop-
ping from her shoulders. What a complex creature
his soon-to-be wife was—so beautiful and delicate
on the outside, so very strong on the inside. That
strength continued to take him by surprise. She
was not afraid to fight, not afraid to live without
comforts, not afraid even to sew him up. Whether
she knew it or not, her own strength had given him
strength during that difficult procedure.

Now, he was taking her home to Pendennys, the
place he loved most in the world, to share with her.
If he wasn't careful, he'd turn this into a fairy-tale
ending. This was no fairy tale.

Marrying Lilya meant marrying her legacy. He
had only abstractly understood that before. The
shooting had not driven home what that meant so
much as the flight to Cornwall had, watching Lilya's
efficiency closing up the town house, sending off the
staff for their protection and hers, hiding the valuables against fear of destruction. To know that she

thought of doing such tasks told him much about the nature of her life before England. It also served as a precursor about what he might expect later. This would become his life, too.

He prayed it wouldn't come to that—that they would not be bundling up children in the dead of night to flee Pendennys, perhaps never to return, with a travelling trunk and necessities tucked beneath a carriage seat. It was the stuff of nightmares. What had happened in London showed him that he must prepare for such an eventuality, even if it never happened. He had to act and think as if it would. Well, so be it. Better the devil you know. Such an endeavour would be far worse if he didn't see it coming. He'd choose organised chaos over random panic any day. Perhaps this was the reason he had fine horses in his stable at Pendennys and a superb travelling coach. He would see to the rest of the arrangements immediately. He would encourage Val to do the same, although he fervently hoped having Lilya out of Val's home would protect them, that they'd be left alone entirely.

But as much as he wanted to avoid it, he could not leave Lilya alone to face it. He cared for her more than he'd planned on caring for another. That was all he was willing to admit to. From the moment he'd seen her back, he'd been fighting the attraction. He was still fighting, but he was losing.

They passed the stone fence marking the entrance

to Pendennys lands. He toed Lilya gently with his boot. 'Wake up. We're nearly there.'

'Nearly there,' Lilya echoed sleepily, peeking out the window with a soft smile. 'I like the sound of that.'

Beldon did, too. Perhaps now she could relax back in safe surroundings. He had not failed to notice the mental toll the journey had taken on her in addition to the physical exigencies of fast travel. She always awoke with a start as if expecting trouble at every moment. Beldon highly suspected she had another knife strapped to her leg for security. And that she slept with the diamond on her person. Sometimes when he watched her sleep, her hand would caress something near her hip. That would definitely have to go. Beldon had no intention of sharing his bed with anything else but Lilya. Once she felt safe again, they'd find a place for her to keep the diamond.

Lilya was suddenly all feminine alarm. 'I must look a fright, four days on the road and just awake from sleeping.' She frantically rummaged through a satchel, searching for a brush.

Beldon laughed; he couldn't help it. It was a splendid sight to see Lilya worried over something trivial like her hair after a week of worrying over something much more.

She skewered him with a stare. 'What are you laughing at?'

'I'm laughing at you,' he admitted with a grin.

Lilya's only recourse was a loud 'humph'.

Lilya raised her arms up to brush the back of her hair, her breasts pushed forwards by the motion. Beldon's body stirred in excited possibility. If she kept that up, they'd make all haste available. His body's message was clear. He was nearly recovered in many ways. He'd been without her for too long.

She caught his gaze and blushed. 'Don't look at me like that.'

'Like what?' He feigned innocence.

'Like you want to devour me.'

'But I do.'

'You're wounded.' She tied her hair in a blue ribbon she'd rummaged from her bag.

'My arm is wounded, not my—'

'You're insatiable!' she scolded, cutting off the end of his reply.

'And you're a siren, Lilya Stefanov,' he countered easily, stretching his legs out in front of him. It felt good to flirt, good to not be in constant pain from his arm, good to think about what might be waiting for him at the end of the evening.

Pendennys gleamed in sunset splendour before them, the smooth sandstone walls awash in the rosy hues of dusk, two storeys of windows reflecting the last light of day. Lilya had been to Pendennys before on a few occasions, but never had its magnificence struck her so deeply. Today she saw it through different eyes. No longer did she view it through the lens of a temporary visitor. This was to be her home and she was to be its mistress, a thought that inspired awe and trepidation. What a responsibility lay before her. She hoped she was up to the task. For it was clear that Beldon held these acres of England more dear than any other.

The carriage rolled to a halt in the drive and they eagerly got out, knowing this was the last stop. After days of travelling and sitting, they would not have to get back inside.

Beldon led her inside, grinning wolfishly as he said, 'The only thing I regret is that my shoulder won't permit me to carry you over the threshold.'

Lilya laughed. 'That's purely a western European superstition.' But surreptitiously, she carefully picked up the hem of her gown anyway to prevent anything that might resemble tripping as they crossed the threshold. Superstition or not, they would have enough bad luck as it was.

There was organisation and official introductions to take care of in the main foyer. Then it was time for a long looked-for bath. There'd only been the most rudimentary of washing on the road and Lilya sank into a steaming tub with alacrity at the first moment possible.

She'd been given the baroness's room since it made little sense to unpack her things in a guest room just to move them after the wedding. The bar-

oness's room was well appointed, all done in blues
and yellows. Most especially, Lilya noted, the baroness's room connected to the baron's room. She'd
spotted the door to Beldon's chambers immediately,
a warm heat taking root at the prospect. She could
hear him next door, talking with his valet as he carefully prepared to bathe without getting his shoulder
wet. She could not make out the words precisely, but
the rise and fall of his voice through the wall was a
heady domestic melody—one that could easily lull
her into a sense of complacency and security. Her
house, her soon-to-be husband getting naked in the
room next to her's…

She closed her eyes, imagining him stripping off
his trousers, his firm buttocks bending and flex-
ing with his movements, his chest bare of his shirt,
his nipples perhaps erect from the slight chill of the
room. Of course it wouldn't be quite like that. With
his shoulder, it would be a bit hard to bend and flex,
but his body would be magnificent none the less. He
wanted her. She'd seen it in his eyes in the carriage
as he'd flirted. She wanted him, too, the memory of
their love-making in the drawing room foremost on
her mind. To claim the glorious rapture it brought
again was a heady temptation.

Lilya relaxed in the luxury of her bath until the
water cooled. Then she dressed in a silky rose-
coloured robe and gave herself over to the maid who
combed out her wet hair, all the while waiting for

Beldon, her eyes going periodically and ridiculously to the connecting door. They were not husband and wife yet. He could not come through that door with her maid present.

She would go to him. A small tremor shuddered through her at the thought. If they were going to play at a marriage, they might as well play at all of it. There was no sense denying themselves the more pleasant aspects of their ruse. She might not be able to claim his love, but she could claim the pleasures of his body.

The maid put down the brush and Lilya dismissed her for the night. The door had barely shut behind the maid before Lilya was opening a door of her own. She put her ear to the door, listening to make sure he was alone. Hearing nothing, she turned the handle.

The scene in the master's bedroom was perfect domestic bliss. A warm fire burned, the bed was turned back for the night and Beldon sat at a small writing table, dressed in a silk banyan, jotting in a journal with his good hand, the remnants of his bath clinging damply to the ends of his hair, darkening the chestnut strands. The only thing marring the scene was the stark whiteness of the sling Beldon wore, a reminder that his world wasn't restful at all.

Beldon looked up from his writing and closed his book, his eyes roaming her body appreciatively. She grew warm from the perusal. She'd gone to her lover's room clad in nothing but a dressing gown. There could be no mistaking her intentions or expectations.

'Is there something you want, Lilya?' How did he do that—take a polite question and deliver it with the seductiveness of a lover just as he had bowed over her hand at the ball and left her tingling with want? He rose from his chair and moved towards her.

'You know what I want.' She opted to play the siren.

He grinned wickedly. 'I want to hear you say it.'

Chapter Sixteen

'I want you.' The words were surprisingly difficult to say. It would have been easier to simply unbelt her robe and ask without the words. The words made it so much more intimate, more binding. She'd wanted him for days, to be honest. She'd wanted to feel his strength, wanted to feel the power of his arms, to know that he was all right.

Then he kissed her, his mouth hot and full over hers, and all of her pent-up excitement was released, given free rein. Oh, how her body had missed this during the days on the road, through the long hours of worry over Beldon's shoulder.

Her excitement made her bold. His arm prohibited him from taking sole control. She would use that to her advantage. She slid to her knees, parting his banyan to find him already thoroughly aroused and naked beneath. She tentatively rose up to take him in her mouth, wanting to kiss him intimately the way he had kissed her breasts. Surely there must be a male equivalent for what he'd done for her. Beldon drew a sharp breath, his good hand anchoring in her hair, but there was no mistaking the motions for anything other than pleasure and it buoyed her confidence. He was all salt and moisture on her tongue.

'Lilya.' Beldon's husky voice demanded her attention. 'We must move this to the bed if you want me to last any longer.'

She rose with a smile and held out her hand. 'Come to bed then, my love.'

Beldon's eyes gleamed with a husbandly possession, a dangerous smile curving his lips. 'I had no idea you were such a temptress.'

She took him astride on the bed out of deference to his shoulder. His blue eyes glittered up at her, desire riding him hard. He bucked hard against her, and she cried out at the force of him pulsing deep inside her. Then they were rushing together into the peace of a well-sated oblivion.

Beldon was gone when she awoke. From the coolness of the sheets, it appeared he'd been up and about for a while. From the amount of daylight streaming in through the curtains, she should have been, too. She'd spent the entire night in Beldon's bed. She really ought not to have. They weren't married yet and there were the servants to consider. That gave her a cause for worry. Lilya scrambled from the bed, taking a moment to gather up her robe where it had fallen the night before, and slipped into her room.

Being back in her chamber wasn't good enough. Lilya immediately recognised her bed didn't look slept in. Hastily she pulled out a nightgown and slid beneath the covers, laughing at the silliness. What lengths had to be achieved to preserve appearances! Really, Beldon should have awakened her when he got up.

Then again, if he had, they might still be in bed. What a delicious thought that was. She'd become quite the wanton under his expert tutelage. Lilya suppressed a giggle and rang for a maid.

'There, you look right pretty, my lady.' The maid stepped back from the dressing table to survey the simple style she'd fashioned for Lilya. 'I hope it will do, me not being a real lady's maid.'

Lilya smiled in the mirror. 'It will be fine. You did a lovely job.' Frankly, the reflection in the mirror stunned her. The woman in the mirror looked positively radiant. 'Lovely' was too tame a word. She'd never looked 'radiant' before. Lovely, yes. Beautiful, yes. But radiant? True, the hairstyle looked nice. There was something else in her reflection, too, a softness that hadn't been there before. She'd slept

mouth. 'They have been dismissed. We will not be bothered for a while.'

He blew against her curls, the warmth of his breath a subtle reminder that she was already damp for him. He lowered his mouth to her and she bit her lip against the flood of sensations that swamped her upon contact. This was a heady elixir indeed to be caressed in such an intimate manner. She had not guessed at the possibility or at the intensity of its outcome. She shuddered against him in replete satisfaction, aware only now that her hands had gripped the arms of her chair with enough force to leave the imprint of her nails behind in the delicate wood.

Beldon looked up, his eyes smoky with his own desire. 'And that, my dear, is why we need a chaperon.'

Philippa arrived late that afternoon with her family in tow and luggage wagon to follow. Even though Valerian's home was only two hours away, they would be in residence until after the wedding. 'Proprieties must be observed,' Philippa said with a smile, kissing Beldon on the cheek in sisterly affection and sweeping into the hall. Of course, they both exclaimed over Beldon's injury. But by implicit agreement, no one mentioned the business with the diamond beyond that.

Lilya knew they were all waiting and hoping, as she was, that Christoph would give up the search, that he'd believe she didn't hold the diamond, that no keeper of the diamond would marry so publicly. He knew where she was so it had to be a good sign that he hadn't come yet. It just had to be because with every day that passed, Lilya knew it would be harder and harder to leave.

The wedding neared. Philippa had declared it would take ten days to put together a decent affair and Lilya had checked off each day as a blessing when it passed without complication.

Each day was a chance to learn about the handsome man she'd wed at the end of the week. For all that he knew of her, she knew very little of him beyond his connection to Valerian and she found she wanted to know. She supposed she knew the things that mattered: he was honourable, he was loyal. She couldn't have contemplated marriage if he hadn't been those things. Running would have been preferable to marriage with a man who was untrustworthy. But she wanted to know the little things: his favorite colour, the way he took his tea, the foods he liked. If she was going to be a wife, she wanted to be a good one.

That meant learning the estate as well as the man, and Beldon was eager to teach her. Pendennys was at its best in the summer and it was obvious Beldon delighted in showing it to her. The best days were spent under the sunshine roaming the estate with him, always taking care not to exhaust him without him noticing. He hated being fussed over, but she'd do it anyway.

'They all love you, you know,' she told him one late afternoon walking back from the vicar's. 'Everyone I've met has had to tell me all the things you've done for them. Mrs Ford said you put on a new roof for her a few winters back. Mrs Garner said you bought her a cow so she could sell milk when her husband couldn't work any more.' Lilya sneaked a peek at Beldon from beneath the rim of her bonnet.

'Don't be embarrassed. You've done well here. Be proud.' It was illuminating to see him in this light. She could add 'proud, responsible landowner' to the list of attributes that described her soon-to-be husband. She'd heard, of course, how much Pendennys meant to him. She had not fully understood what that meant until she'd walked the land with him. This was his life, his absolute everything. His hard work, his sweat, his money, was evident in the landscape in so many ways.

They passed by the cemetery just beyond the church and stopped to rest, leaning on the iron fencing. 'No one will ever take Pendennys from me again,' Beldon said, looking out over the gravestones.

'Not even me,' Lilya murmured, unaware she'd spoken the thought out loud.

'What was that?' Beldon turned his head sharply to look at her. 'What did you say?'

It was the first time the diamond had intruded since their arrival. They'd been careful to focus only on the present, to keep the future precisely where it was—in the future.

'Nothing.'

'No, you said, "Not even me",' he argued. 'You're to be my wife. That's different and it's not at all what I meant.'

Lilya chose to let the remark pass. It wasn't different, but quarrelling would serve no purpose. He was just as stubborn as she was. She turned her attentions to the cemetery. 'Your father still has you in his thrall. You worry about being like him,' Lilya divined, following his gaze. 'I did not know him, obviously, but I can't believe he was a terrible man. Val speaks kindly of him.'

Beldon shook his head, lifting a foot to rest on the low rung of the fence. 'He was a good man. We all loved him and he loved us. But he let his love betray us.'

Lightning could not have struck more brightly. There it was, the reason for the aloof hauteur of the man she'd met in London; emotions must not be engaged, at least not over the long term. He didn't trust himself to love. Caring could only extend so far before it crossed the boundaries of love. Of course, Beldon loved his nephew, loved his sister. But they were ultimately Valerian's responsibilities. They were safe to love. But a wife? A woman who claimed his heart? That woman would be the least safe of all.

'I do not think you are him, with or without your armour,' Lilya offered.

'I don't have armour.'

'Yes, you do. It's your manners and your unfailing politeness. It's hard to penetrate the surface of all the perfection you walk around with.'

'You make it sound like I'm a prig,' Beldon groused.

'Not at all,' Lilya cried. 'That's your charm. You have pulled it off with *élan.* The ladies all wonder what is beyond that handsome face of yours, what secrets lie beneath all that immutable perfection.' Lilya gave him a sly look. 'Surely you're aware of the ladies and their attentions?'

Beldon chuckled. 'I have noticed I get my fair share of attention on occasion.'

'You smile more in the country. I like that. It was one of the things I noticed about you first.'

'You've have mentioned it before.' Beldon leaned close to her ear. Whatever he said, it was going to be wicked. 'Do you want to know what I noticed about you first?'

'Don't say my eyes. Everyone in England says my eyes.'

Beldon drew back for a moment in an exaggerated pose of thoughtful contemplation. 'Hmm, well, yes.

I can see where some might say that. They are rather nice, all dark and tipped up a little at the edges like a cat's.'

'Ahem.' Lilya cleared her throat, unwilling to let a pending compliment get away. 'You were going to tell me what it was you noticed first?'

Beldon grinned, letting his eyes dance with mischief. 'It was your back, my dear.'

'My back?'

'Yes, and tomorrow night I will show you exactly what I was thinking when I saw it.'

Tomorrow night. Just the thought made her weak in the knees. It would be their wedding night. It did not matter they'd spent every night they could in his bed. Tomorrow would be their first night as man and wife. Tomorrow, everything would change. They would be bound together for ever in the eyes of God for better or worse. Please, Lilya thought. Let it be for the better.

Beldon waited until the house fell silent before going downstairs to his study. The hall clock read one in the morning. Technically it was his wedding day, although the sun wouldn't be up for hours. *No one* would be up for hours. That was fine with him. The house had been bustling the past few days with preparations. He had preparations of his own to make and he wanted to be alone for them.

Beldon sat down behind the wide desk that had

served four generations of Pendennys barons and pulled out writing materials. He dipped his pen, drew a deep breath and began to write: *I, Beldon Elliot Stratten, the current Baron Pendennys, being of sound mind and body, do hereby certify this document to be my last will and testament...*

Dire words, to be sure, for a man to pen on the morning of his wedding. It reminded him of the old tradition of Scottish brides beginning their winding sheets for burial the day after their weddings. But if anything happened, he wanted to be prepared. He wanted Lilya and Pendennys to be safe. The estate would go to young Alex, Philippa's son, in the event he died without an heir.

Beldon finished the document and sanded it before setting it aside. He reached for another fresh sheet. He hesitated a moment before writing the bold letters across the top: *Our escape in the event of emergency.* This list was harder to write than the will. What happened if he couldn't protect Lilya at Pendennys? What happened if the day came when they had to flee in order to save their lives? Could he simply walk away from the estate for Lilya? He'd promised himself once years ago when he'd first taken on the estate that he'd not let it go as long as there was breath in his body. He'd have to be dead to part with Pendennys; it was his legacy and it had become his life.

Beldon paused and looked down at the sheet of

paper, a new thought coming to him, one that might save them for ever when the time came. If he was willing. What would he give up for Lilya? How far would he go for love?

Love. Beldon sighed. He'd tried so very hard to avoid it and it had found him anyway. He was in love with Lilya. He wasn't sure when it had happened. He couldn't look at a calendar and circle the day. Perhaps he'd loved her the moment he'd spotted her in the Fitzsimmons' ballroom. Perhaps he'd loved her the day she'd shown him the diamond, or the day they'd first made love. He didn't know. Love had been very stealthy in this case, creeping up slowly, disguising itself in the cloak of duty and the mask of honour.

Yes, he loved the woman who would wed him tomorrow and he'd stand with her even if it cost him everything.

Chapter Seventeen

Happy-ever-after started today! Lilya's room was a flurry of activity, full of maids bustling about with clothes and combs and jewellery. Philippa sat serenely in the window seat, holding the baby and directing the chaos with a well-placed instruction here and there. Lilya hardly minded. She'd been up early in spite of a late night. Supper had been delayed on Philippa's behalf. She'd spent the day organising the decorating of the little chapel.

Lilya had yet to see the results. As the bride she'd been shooed away, the villagers laughingly declaring it was bad luck for the bride to decorate for her own wedding. But there'd been finishing touches to put on the wedding breakfast that would be held after the ceremony this morning and Lilya had been busy with them when she and Beldon had returned to the house.

She'd slept surprisingly well and taken a hearty walk this morning, glorying in the natural beauty of Pendennys by sunrise. Now, there was nothing left to do but dress and make her way to church.

She was really going to do this. Her nerves started to rise as the dress was lifted over her head. Her wedding! She was going to be married, something she'd once thought of as an impossibility.

The gown was an ivory confection Philippa had brought from home. Lilya's original wedding dress was languishing unclaimed in London, a casualty of her hasty departure. But Lilya loved this wedding gown even more. It had belonged to Valerian's mother and an earlier age. But it was done in simple elegance without excessive trims, much like Lilya's own gowns. The fuller skirt of a bygone era belled out delightfully when Lilya took a practice step. She felt like a fairy queen.

Philippa laughed as Lilya twirled experimentally in front of the long pier glass. 'Our skirts are getting wider again, in a few years this will be all the style. Everyone will say how à la mode Lady Pendennys is.'

'Lady Pendennys.' Lilya bit her lip, nerves warring with excitement.

Philippa came to stand with her, looking at them both in the mirror. 'You'll be splendid. Beldon will be a good husband to you and you are not indifferent to him. You will find your way together. Now, you'll really be family although we've never thought of you as less.'

'You've all been so good to me.' Lilya sniffed, tears threatening at Philippa's kind words.

'No tears,' Philippa said briskly, glancing about until she found what she was looking for. 'There it is.' She picked up a small box. 'My pearls. I wore them the day I married Val and I'd like you to have them to wear today.'

'Oh, Philippa, I couldn't...' Lilya began.

Philippa smiled. 'Something old, something new, something borrowed, something blue, a silver sixpence in your shoe. It's a wedding rhyme,' she explained. 'You have Val's mother's dress, so that's something old, my pearls are something borrowed. It's all for good luck, really.'

'Sometimes I feel I can use all the luck I can get.' Lilya laughed, looking about the room. 'Hmm, something new and something blue?'

'Your bouquet!' Philippa chimed in. 'It will have blue forget-me-nots in it. Now for something new—the sixpence will be easy.'

They rummaged through Lilya's things and came up with a new handkerchief that had never been used. 'This is what happens when you don't plan your trousseau,' Philippa scolded with a laugh.

'There.' Lilya tucked the small handkerchief into

her glove. Later, she could wrap it around her bouquet and hold it during the ceremony. 'Now I have all the luck possible.' She sobered a bit, standing still to let the maids arrange the long gossamer veil on her head. 'I hope Beldon doesn't regret this.'

'Oh, my dear, why would he?' Philippa sobered, too. 'You needn't worry on that account. You're not still worried about the diamond, are you? Beldon will not let that stand between you. It's been two weeks and there's been no sign of…' Philippa paused here, unwilling to speak the name. 'Agyros,' she said at last with a sigh. 'Perhaps he is persuaded you didn't have it.'

'Beldon loves this place, Philippa. These last days, I've had a chance to see him here. Pendennys is his soul. He's spent his adult life making this place what it is. He'd told me about your father. But I'd not really understood how much this place meant to Beldon until we arrived. This is all he's ever wanted.'

Lilya whispered her greatest fear. 'What if he has to choose? What if marrying me forces him to choose?'

'He won't have to choose, just as you didn't have to choose the diamond or a happy marriage. Sometimes we only *think* we have to choose.' Philippa squeezed her hand, bringing back the earlier gaiety. 'It's time to go and I know Constantine is in the carriage waiting. Take one last look at Lilya Stefanov.

When you come back you'll be Lady Pendennys, for ever.'

Lilya smiled at the woman in the mirror. She hoped it would be that easy. Perhaps as Lady Pendennys she could work out who she might have been if she hadn't been the keeper.

An open carriage waited for her in the drive, Constantine already aboard for the short trip to the church. He was dressed in a dark suit and his black hair combed for the occasion. He looked like a very mature ten-year-old. He looked, Lilya realised, like their father and she wondered that she hadn't seen the resemblance sooner: the dark hair, the hazel-green eyes and the sharp Stefanov nose that gave their faces their regal look. Constantine was growing up, no longer the baby she'd raised since that terrible night in Negush. She'd been no older than Constantine was now when the diamond and he had both been put into her care. Constantine, of course, was thrilled she was marrying Beldon. He adored Valerian's friend and the fact that his sister wouldn't be living too far away.

Lilya got into the carriage, sparing a final thought for those who weren't with her on this most special day: her brother Alexei, her mother, her aunt, her father. They'd want her to be happy today. They wouldn't want her to dwell on what might have been.

Beldon would understand the need to take a moment and honour them. His parents weren't here either. He'd been a good son. If it had been his choice, he'd have wanted his parents to see him wed and bring the next generation to Pendennys. On her walk this morning, she'd seen a fresh posy of flowers at the cemetery where they'd stopped the day before. Some time during the busy excitement, he, too, had found time to make his peace with the past just as she was doing right now.

She squeezed Constantine's hand as Philippa settled into the seat beside her and they were off to church beneath the clear blue sky of a Cornwall summer day.

The road to the church was lined with well-wishers and all those who couldn't fit into the little chapel. They would all be welcomed at the wedding breakfast afterwards, the doors of Pendennys flung open for all to share in the occasion. Beldon was a well-liked man and everyone was eager to share in his happiness.

At the chapel, Lilya was helped down from the carriage, a hush falling over those standing nearest the door, a whisper rippling through the crowd. 'The bride, the bride is here.' Philippa slipped past her with Constantine to take her place up front as a witness. Valerian waited inside to escort her up the aisle. 'Be sure to look around and note the decorations,' Val whispered. 'You'll want to remember this day in all its detail for the rest of your life.'

Lilya did her best to take in the flower garlands

that draped the pews, but she could not do it justice. Her eyes were for the man who waited for her at the end of her walk. Broad-shouldered and tall, the sun sparking his chestnut hair into deep rich honeyed hues, Beldon Stratten waited for her, ready to bind his life with hers.

The service passed in solemn awe, Beldon's grip firm on her hands, and she was glad for his strength. At last, Beldon kissed her, sealing their union, and she welcomed it until Valerian coughed discreetly in suggestion that the union was sealed quite well enough for now. Lilya stifled a giggle, but she could not stifle the smile that spread across her face. Euphoric relief swamped her. Tension ebbed from her. It was well and truly done now. *What God has joined together let no man tear asunder.* A gold band glinted on her hand in reminder of that. She wanted to laugh and dance and sing. Everyone else did, too; weddings brought out the best in people and the crowds of people following the carriage to Pendennys were merry. Beldon threw the customary coins for the children and there was much joking and jostling as children scrambled for the pennies.

Pendennys was ready for them, white canopies dotting the lawn ready for guests. Tables groaned with all nature of Cornish delicacies conjured up miraculously with only a few days' notice. To Lilya's delight, there were fiddlers, too. There would be dancing—not the dancing found in London's ball-rooms, but good hearty country dancing.

It was a day of days. Lilya danced with Beldon and with Val and then Beldon again until his arm began to ache. It was easy to forget he'd been injured almost three weeks ago.

When they weren't dancing, Beldon took her hand and wound their way through the tables to visit with the guests. Beldon knew them all by name and history. He talked agriculture with the farmers and ore with the miners.

But even with the entertainment and the plentiful food, the guests demonstrated uncommonly good sense and began making their farewells as late afternoon came on. It was time for the married couple to be on their own, and themselves as well. Lilya had no doubt many of them would go home and spend the evening remembering wedding days past.

'You're blushing,' Beldon said quietly in her ear.

'I was thinking how these happy people will go home and perhaps do a little recalling of their own weddings.'

Beldon arched an eyebrow. 'Or anticipating future weddings.'

She tilted her head up to consider the man beside her. 'Well, who can blame them? It's a marvellous thing what a man and a woman can do together.'

'I take it you're ready to go inside, Lady Pendennys.' Beldon laughed.

'More than ready,' Lilya answered softly.

Someone had paid special attention to his bedchamber. Candles had been freshly lit against the early shadows of evening. A small fire had been laid, the covers of the bed turned back and sprinkled with rose petals. Champagne was chilling, waiting in an ice bucket. A small table had been set up with cold slices of meat and bread and a bowl of fresh strawberries. His banyan and Lilya's things had been laid out. Someone had guessed rightly they wouldn't want the assistance of a valet or maid tonight, but also that the night was young and they'd be hungry before it was over.

Beldon expertly worked the cork of the champagne until it gave a soft pop. He poured two glasses and handed one to Lilya. 'A toast, my dear, to the best day of our lives, and many more to come.'

He drank, his eyes never leaving Lilya's face. Marriage agreed with her already. Her eyes glowed, dark coals lit with an appreciation of life. He'd seen her start to relax, start to believe in the peace he could offer her during the past weeks. Whatever he could or couldn't give her, he would give her peace. He owed her that.

He was acutely aware she had not sought marriage. She had not sought him. And yet here she was.

He had no illusions as to why she'd married him. But it didn't have to stay that way. There was no reason they couldn't grow into a companionable marriage. Goodness knew their bed sport was headed in the right direction. And she already had his admiration. She'd raised her brother, being no more than a child herself; she'd crossed Europe on her own. His wife was a woman of uncommon courage. If she could come so far on her own, she could certainly muster the courage to build a real marriage here with him.

'I have something for you.' Beldon went to a drawer and pulled out a long green velvet case. 'This is your official wedding present,' he announced with a flourish, taking her glass from her so she could sit and open the box.

'Oh, my. They're beautiful.' Lilya's face was a study of awe. 'Are these the family jewels? Shouldn't they be Philippa's?'

'No, Philippa has her own and the St Just jewellery, too,' Beldon assured her.

But even amid her protests, Beldon could see that she liked them. The Pendennys emeralds were exquisite. She held up a diamond-and-emerald parure to catch the firelight. 'This is magnificently cut.'

'Here, try it on.' Beldon gently set it on her head and stepped back. She was a queen in it, regal and commanding. He would have chosen this piece of jewellery for her even if it hadn't been in the family vault. There were other pieces, too, and she held each one up, admiring them in turn.

'Thank you, Beldon.'

'You're welcome. Some of the pieces are older and they're a bit heavy. We can have them reset in something more fashionable the next time we're in London, or perhaps a jeweller in Truro could do the work.'

'I am in no hurry.' Lilya set aside the last of the jewels. 'Come, help me with my gown.' She turned, presenting her back to him.

Beldon gave a hearty laugh. 'It's a good thing we retired early. There's enough buttons here to keep me busy all night. Good Lord, this would frustrate any groom.'

Or tantalise, Beldon soon amended, his fingers adroitly handling the little silk-covered buttons than ran the length of her back—Lilya's delectable back. He spread the fabric apart, revealing the smooth expanse of skin, and laid a trail of kisses down the length of her spine. 'I've wanted to do this since the first time I saw you in London.' He heard the huskiness of his own voice, low and primal already. This woman could arouse him instantly and to limitless depths.

He pushed the gown off her shoulders and down to her hips, making short work of the undergarments beneath, his lips at her bare shoulder. 'I didn't recognise you at first in London. I couldn't see your face, but I saw an elegant woman with great poise and I wondered why this woman hadn't been on my list. How could I have missed such a stunning creature?' His list, his stupid list, seemed a long time ago in a foolish lifetime. How could he ever have thought he'd be happy with a Lady Eleanor Braithmore?

'All because of my back?' Lilya leaned against him, careful of his dratted shoulder.

'For starters.' Beldon placed a kiss at the base of her neck, noting how her pulse jumped at the sweet contact, her breasts filled his hands and he languidly caressed a nipple into readiness. 'It didn't take long to realise you were far more than a sum of your beauty, Lilya.' He was aware she'd shifted her hips ever so slightly and the dress slid over the slim curves of her hips to the floor, leaving her naked to his gaze.

Lilya turned in his arms, her breasts pressed against his shirted chest. She was going to tease him, he could see it in her eyes. 'I thought you said it was my back you loved.'

'I wanted to seduce you by candlelight. Your back conjured up all nature of erotic fantasies.' Beldon waltzed her to the bed until her knees hit the frame and she fell back on to the rose petals.

He stepped away to give her a full view as he undressed. Perhaps not the most graceful undressing with one stiff arm, but the intent was there. Tonight he was her man entirely. Beldon shrugged out of his shirt and kicked off his trousers, sliding beneath the cool sheets with her. She was ready for him, meeting him with legs parted, intuitively knowing that on this night, he would do the seducing. Tonight, he needed to do the possessing, to join with other males in the ageless ritual of taking one's bride.

He rose above her, bracing his arm with a pillow, ignoring the strain. He took her mouth in a fierce kiss and plunged into her welcome depths, letting her legs close about him, holding him as her hips rose to match the cadence of his body. Lilya gasped beneath him, her pleasure nearly reached. He surged once more, his body gathering for a final release as he brought them to completion, pouring his seed, pouring his soul into this woman with the realisation that, on his wedding night, he was falling in love with his bride, the one thing above all else he'd sworn not to do.

Above all else, he would retrieve that diamond or die trying. The latest letter from the *Filiki* confirmed all other suspects had turned up nothing. Lilya had the diamond. It was what Christoph had wished for. He would be the one to return triumphant. But the *Filiki* had also noted their disappointment with his slow progress after the promises he'd made them earlier in May. May seemed ages ago now. May had been a month of promise. He'd found Lilya. He'd put his courtship gambit in motion. Then Beldon Stratten had emerged and obliterated his plans in one fell evening of discovery.

Now it was July. Lilya and that dratted Pendennys had slipped through his fingers. They were married. The London newspapers had announced two weeks ago that Baron Pendennys had married Lilya Stefanov. It was a small consolation that he knew where she was, where she'd been all along. There was no mention of a wedding trip. Lulling her into complacency hadn't been a bad idea. Unaware was unprepared. But it did come with some trade-offs. Now he'd have to go to Pendennys's territory and play the invader. In London there'd been a sense of neutrality.

Well, best be done with it. He would take a few days to plan and make travel arrangements. Even if she didn't have the diamond, he had unfinished business with them. This was personal now. Pendennys and she had made him look like a foolish suitor.

He stood and stretched. This time was for keeps.

Chapter Eighteen

The fashionable world would have found it odd that Beldon had not whisked his bride away on a six-month wedding trip to the south of Italy or to some other destination, but Lilya was perfectly happy to stay ensconced at Pendennys and wile away the rest of the summer.

They might be at home, but that did not put a dampener on the early high spirits of their marriage. While being home meant there was the business of running the house and the estate, there was still plenty of time for picnics and long rides. No one expected them to entertain yet, so they had their lives to themselves, with time to work out the companionship of daily living.

'When do you suppose we have to give our first dinner party?' Lilya picked idly at grass stems, sitting with her skirts tucked about her on their picnic blanket.

Beldon lay back on the blanket, hands tucked behind his head, looking up at the sky. 'Not until the autumn. I think we could put it off until October.' He looked over at her, those eyes of his dancing. 'You're not tired of me already, are you? Ready to get back to the social whirl?' he teased.

Lilya rolled her eyes and smiled. 'Hardly.' She flung her arms wide. 'I could never tire of this or of you.' She shrugged. 'People have been very good to leave us to ourselves. I know people are trying hard not to impose. I wonder how long they'll be patient before we'll need to fully take up our duties. I will miss having you to myself when they do.' She'd enjoyed this time alone with him more than she could ever express in words.

Beldon rolled to his side. 'Ouch!' He sat up, wincing.

'Is it your shoulder?'

It had been a month now since he'd been hurt and, with the exception of an occasional twinge, he seemed well healed.

Beldon grinned and shook his head. 'No, just a reminder that I have something for you, something I've been meaning to give you for a while. I keep thinking I'll wait for the right time, but I can't quite decide when that will be. In the meanwhile, I've impaled my hip on it.' Beldon reached into his coat pocket and pulled out a small box.

'I don't need presents, Beldon.' She was coming to find out he was always full of surprises. There'd been a well-trained mare for her in the stables last week. There'd been a shipment of books from Hatchard's a few days ago. Now this. He was the most thoughtful of gift-givers, selecting items that would suit her perfectly.

She untied the ribbon, recognising the signature colours of the jewellers' at the Burlington Arcade. She opened the lid and tears threatened. 'The bracelet.' She gave a breathless gasp, turning the bracelet in the sun, letting the light spark off the tourmaline. 'It's lovely. Help me with the clasp, I want to put it on.'

Beldon fastened the circlet around her wrist. 'I thought to use it as an engagement present, but it was rather difficult when you wouldn't accept my proposal outright.'

'It's hard to accept outright when one is not asked outright,' she replied drily.

'Hush, you're interrupting, minx. *Then* I thought to use it as a wedding gift, but there were the family jewels to give. I thought a two-week anniversary is as good a cause to celebrate as any. Otherwise, I could be stuck carrying this around until Christmas and who knows what other bruises that could result in.'

Lilya lifted her wrist, watching the play of light on the gems.

'I've been told tourmaline signifies devotion and balance in a marriage.' Beldon reached for her hand, drawing her to him. She came willingly, lying down close to him on the blanket, the scent of his morning soap mixed with the smells of grass and summer.

'You've brought me balance, Lilya.' He pushed back a length of hair from her face, his warm hand cupping the curve of her jaw.

She smiled. 'You remembered why a woman likes jewellery.'

'Yes, you see, I can be taught.' Beldon chuckled, a low sensual sound near her ear. They weren't going to be talking about jewellery and fine sentiments much longer. His hands were already working the buttons of the linen blouse she'd worn beneath her riding jacket when they'd ridden out that morning. She wiggled against him, a tremor of excitement racing through her at the prospect of making love outdoors. And why not? Other than the horses picketed nearby, there was no one to see.

Suddenly Beldon tensed and pushed her away. He heaved himself up, looking around.

'What is it?' Lilya struggled to sit up.

'I heard something, someone.' Beldon rose to his feet and called out. 'Halloo, we're over here.' He gave an exaggerated wave.

Lilya fumbled hastily with her buttons. A stable

boy from Pendennys rode into view, his horse lathered from a hard ride. Anxiety took her. Something had happened. She rose to stand beside Beldon, her hand immediately slipping into his. It was a sign of her complacency that her first thought had been for a tenant, perhaps a farmer hurt out in the fields.

'My lord…' the boy was breathless '…there's been an accident at the stable. The head groom, Bassett, he tried to stop it, but…'

Tried to stop it? Those weren't words used to describe an accident. Then Christoph crossed her mind. Lilya didn't wait to hear more. Without conscious thought, she was running to her mare; a swift vault saw her in the saddle, heedless of ankles and high riding skirts. Her mind reeled with thoughts— Christoph was here! She had to get to the diamond. She'd been foolish! She'd felt safe too soon. The diamond was hidden at home; she was without her weapons, her knife tucked in a drawer. She'd thought she'd have some warning, that she would have seen him coming and have time to prepare.

Beldon caught her bridle. 'Lilya! Wait for me.'

'Let me go! There's not a second to lose,' she cried.

'We cannot run headlong into madness,' Beldon argued.

'He's not there, milord.' The stable boy spoke up. 'He's gone now. But he said he'd be back.'

'Then we're already too late!' Lilya was desperate now. She had to get home. She had to get the diamond. Beyond that, she could not think yet. Beldon was up on his horse, giving terse instructions to the stable boy to follow when his horse was rested.

Then they were off, flying over the meadows homewards. Beldon was grim and Lilya wished now that she'd listened to more of the report. What had happened? Was Bassett all right? She urged her horse onwards, taking stone-wall jump after stone-wall jump—there was no time to take the road. Cutting cross-country would be faster.

Pendennys loomed before them at last and they skidded to a halt into an eerily quiet stable yard. Beldon was off his horse instantly. 'Lilya, go to the house and stay there. This is no place for you.' His face was stern, his tone severe. He hardly spared a look for her, leaving her to dismount on her own. She'd seen him like this before in London, commanding and full of authority, a man ready to take on the world—alone.

But Lilya would have none of it. She slid from the mare and ran to catch up. Whatever this tragedy was, it was of her making, she was sure of it. She would not be shielded.

'Where's Bassett?' Beldon asked a pale-faced stable hand.

'We've got him in his room. Mrs Andrews is with him. She's stopped the bleeding.'

'And the horses?'

The other man shook his head. 'They're still in the paddock. We haven't had a chance to move 'em yet.'

'It's all right. It's more important to look after Bassett. There's nothing to be done for them at any rate.'

'It was terrible, milord. The man just walked in here, asked if this was Pendennys and then he started shooting.' The man's voice choked. 'Every horse in the paddock, sir. The new colt, the stallion…'

'What did he look like?' Lilya demanded. 'Was he squat? Beady eyes?' She tried to recall the image of the man who'd shot at Beldon in London.

Beldon rounded on her. 'Lilya, I told you to go to the house. This is not your concern.'

'This *is* my concern! How dare you suggest otherwise!' Lilya railed. Anger and horror warred within her. The man who'd shot Beldon had come here and massacred Beldon's horses. Because of her.

In her anger, she strode towards the paddock, but her gorge rose in her throat before she was halfway there, so intense was the carnage. It was not every horse, many had still been in their stalls, but it was an overt message, meant to warn and terrify. Life was no longer sacred. They would not shoot and miss a second time.

She could not go closer, but she could not look away from one section in particular. The big grey stallion, Thunder, lay over the colt born earlier that spring.

Her legs began to tremble, the horror finally outweighing her anger, her source of strength. A loud desperate sob escaped her; she was going to collapse, she could feel it coming on, but she was powerless to help herself, to stop it. But she didn't fall. Beldon was there, wrapping her in his arms, his anger subdued momentarily by her need for him. He was murmuring nonsense to her.

The stable hand must be with them. She was vaguely conscious of his voice, telling the tale. 'Once Bassett grasped the situation, he charged the man with the gun, but the man had a friend we didn't see right away. It was the friend who shot Bassett, just as cool as you please. Thunder went berserk after that. The old boy was going to protect his mares. He tried herding them to safety, then he tried going after the man. If he could have got out, Thunder would have killed the bastard, would have run the man down. At the end, he took three bullets trying to save the colt. It was over in a matter of minutes, too fast for anyone from the house to help us. By the time they knew what had happened, the men were gone.'

'I'll take Lilya to the house and then I'll come to check on Bassett.' Beldon's tone was quiet, but she was not fooled. He was nowhere near subdued. He was fighting mad and he was going to do something, something that might get him killed.

'I don't need to go to the house. I'm all right now.' Lilya hiccupped, hating her weakness. But she was torn. She wanted to go to the house and check on the diamond, get her knife, arm herself. But she feared if she left Beldon, he'd do something drastic and she'd be left behind.

'Please, let me take you to the house, Lilya.' Beldon was firm and she found no argument to countermand him.

Maids and footmen milled about the front of the house, waiting for news, waiting for something to fill their time in the wake of the tragedy. Beldon knew exactly what to do.

'Tea, please, for Lady Pendennys. She's taken a shock. I'll be back shortly.'

The simple sentence galvanised the staff. Lilya found herself whisked to one of the private family sitting rooms, and tea laid before her, everyone glad for something to do. Her appreciation for her husband rose inestimably. In the face of a tragedy of this magnitude, he was miraculously balancing everyone's needs: the victimised stable hands who'd witnessed the tragedy first-hand, the household staff who wanted to offer comfort and even his own wife's need.

Lilya looked down at the bracelet on her wrist. An hour ago he'd spoken of such things—balance and devotion. He was demonstrating those characteristics this minute. And she was a threat to those

foundations, her very presence a menace to Pendennys, to the core of Beldon's dreams. In the wake of
her happiness it had been convenient to forget.

She sipped at her tea, taking a cue from Beldon's
choices. The servants needed to be busy; the least
she could do was drink the tea and validate their
efforts. The tea helped. Her brain starting function-
ing again, in its old way, the way it used to function
before she'd allowed herself to be something other
than Lilya Stefanov, keeper of the Phanar Diamond.

'Is there anything else you need, milady?' her
maid solicited kindly. How silly it had been to think
she could be other than what she was, to think she
might be someone else besides *Adamao*'s keeper.

'Yes, Sally, there is. I need paper for a note and
someone to ride to St Just's. The viscount must be
told at once.'

Writing supplies were brought immediately and
Lilya wrote with all haste, telling Valerian of the
attack and warning him not to come. Under no cir-
cumstances were he and Philippa to come to them.
But they should prepare themselves, just in case.
Lilya folded the note and handed it to a waiting rider.
'This must go with all speed.'

'What is this, Lilya?' Beldon appeared in the
doorway, letting the rider brush past him. The lines
of his face were grim and his clothes were dusty.

'A note for St Just. Val must know.'

Beldon gave her a curt nod of approval. 'Yes, that's an excellent idea.'

'Tea?' Lilya handed him a cup. 'How is Bassett?'

'He'll recover.' Beldon passed a hand over his mouth. 'We've done what we can to restore order in the stables.'

'Christoph is here,' Lilya said slowly. They had to talk about it. They'd spent a lot of time not talking about it to no good end. He'd come anyway. 'He won't stop until he has the diamond or he's dead.'

Beldon nodded. 'I'd prefer the latter.'

Lilya set down her teacup and met his hard eyes evenly, eyes that had twinkled merrily beside her on a picnic blanket a few hours earlier. 'It would certainly solve things. For now. Until next time.'

'I'll post a watch around Pendennys. He won't get past us again.'

Lilya offered him a wan smile. 'No, he won't.' There wouldn't be a next time if she could help it. She rose. 'You have things to do. You needn't worry about me. I think I'll go up to my room for a bit.'

Lilya went into action the moment she reached the quiet sanctuary of her room. She had to go before he posted the watch. Guards served two purposes, although not always intentionally. They kept people in as much as they kept people out. Beldon was efficient. She wouldn't have much time.

It was no good trying to pretend everything would be all right. Maybe Christoph would give up, or maybe he'd be killed in the trying. It could just as easily be Beldon who was killed. Goodness knew he and Christoph could not co-exist much longer. It would have to be one or the other.

Unless she left.

Then Christoph would have to choose. Certainly he had petty grievances with Beldon, but they did not outweigh his desire, his need, to retrieve the diamond. She could draw him away from Beldon, away from Pendennys.

Away from everything she'd ever wanted when she was brave enough to admit it. Lilya uncovered the diamond from its hiding spot and sank on to the bed. Beldon would hate her for this, and leaving broke her heart. Worse, she feared that for him it would affirm he'd been right to wear his armour, right to stay away from opening up to love.

First instincts were usually right. She should never have deviated from her plan. She should never have married. More than that, she should never have married someone she loved. Lilya rummaged for her travelling cloak with all its inside pockets. She might manage a small bundle of things, but most of what she could take would have to fit in the cloak. No one went for a walk with a valise without arousing suspicion.

The old habits came back, of the times after Negush when she'd lived as best she could, often with relatives who were forced to flee in the night to safety with whatever they could carry. She dressed in layers, selecting the most serviceable of her clothes, wearing a skirt over another skirt. It was summer and layering would be unwelcome weight for a while until she could fashion a better way to carry her things, but she'd be glad of a change of clothes in the long run.

What she needed most was money or things that could be converted into money. Money was portable and it didn't take up space. She had only a little— she could not bring herself to take Philippa's pearls or the Pendennys emeralds—but it would be enough to catch a coach or to buy passage to Ireland. From Ireland there would be boats to America or somewhere else. She'd be less likely to be detected leaving from Ireland. Friends and enemies alike would be watching the English ports. Her success would be in leaving England quickly.

She penned a note to Beldon. It was the only courtesy she could give him. He deserved to know that she'd loved him. That she'd not meant to use him. Perhaps those words would be enough to convince him that he had not been betrayed. The tears started. She squeezed them back. If she let even one tear fall, she'd be lost. Action was better than thought at times, and this was one of those times. If she didn't think about what she was doing, she'd get through it. All she had to do was put one foot in front of the other. She'd concentrate on getting out the front door, then to the parklands, then to the bridle trails that led through the woods. It was unlikely Christoph would know about those trails yet. He'd still be watching the roads. When it was safe, she'd try to get a ride with a farm wagon off to market. Then she'd have time, time to forget that, for a while, she'd had everything.

Beldon returned at dusk, home from posting a watch, dirty and tired. He was emotionally and physically empty. The dream had become a nightmare. Val would have Lilya's message by now. There was some consolation in that, although he hoped it did its job and kept Valerian safely at home.

Decisions had to be made, not so much made as taken. He'd known in his gut this day would come. He'd planned for it even as he'd wanted to believe such plans would be unnecessary. But first, he wanted to steal some heaven with his wife, with Lilya. He wanted one last moment in her arms here at Pendennys before he threw their lives into disarray in a final attempt to save them.

Beldon climbed the stairs, his hand lingering on the polished banister as if his body were committing to memory each touch and feel of a life that was about to end. But his heart had already departed that life. His heart was urging him to the hallway, to Lilya's door. More than he wanted to savour Pendennys, he wanted the comfort of Lilya's arms, and to comfort her in turn.

His thoughts had not been far from her during the day. She knew precisely what had happened and why. The guilt she felt must be paralysing. He wanted desperately to tell her he did not hold her responsible. He feared she might have misunderstood his terseness earlier. He was not angry with her, he was thinking of her safety, of his need to protect her.

Beldon opened her door without a knock. If she was sleeping, he didn't want to wake her. 'Lilya?' he called softly. He stepped inside, shutting the door behind him, expecting to find her in bed. But the bed was empty. Where could she have gone? He yanked the bell pull, summoning her maid.

The maid was quick. She bobbed a curtsy. 'She was up here for a while, said she was going to rest. But she came downstairs and said she was too restless and that she was going for a walk.'

'And you let her?' Beldon snapped. 'After the events of today, you let her go walking on her own?'

The maid looked crestfallen and he regretted his tone. 'Milord, she said she'd stay in the gardens near the house,' she managed to stammer.

'Is she there now?' Beldon's suspicions began to grow.

'I don't know,' the maid said meekly.

'She could be anywhere. Search the house; perhaps she's curled up in a sitting room with a book or has fallen asleep.' Beldon put on a façade of false cheer. 'Meanwhile, I'll search the grounds.' He'd never asked her to reveal the diamond's hiding place. He wished he knew. If the diamond was still here, Lilya was, too. She'd never leave without it. He had no way of knowing, but felt in his bones that she was gone.

Beldon headed downstairs. There was no time to lose. In the study, he unlocked the safe where he kept his pistols. At the front door, he grabbed up his recently discarded cloak. Outside, he cast his eye skywards. The skies were darkening both with the night and rain. It would be wet before long. But Lilya was out there, and he had to find her before Christoph or she did something they'd all regret. Armed only with his pistols and thoughts of finding Lilya, Beldon walked away from all that he knew into a most uncertain night.

Chapter Nineteen

'I am to meet my wife, a woman with long dark hair.' Beldon asked for the fifth time, water flowing in thin steady rivulets from his cloak to the innkeeper's floor. His chase had led him to Falmouth with its harbour and port, confirming his suspicions: Lilya meant to run. Knowing made him impatient. Every minute wasted in another dead end put her further from him. But he was certain she was in Falmouth and he'd search every inn until he found her.

In that at least the soaking rain had been his friend. He knew firsthand the sudden onset of a summer storm had made the coastal road nearly impassable. There would be mudslides before the night was out in places where the road curved sharply along the cliffs of the coast.

This time he was in luck. 'Ah, yes, a lady arrived

earlier. She asked for a private parlour.' Beldon's hopes soared. Lilya would not risk sitting in a public room. She was too smart for that.

The innkeeper led him down a short hall away from the noise of the main room to a small chamber, warm with a fire. Beldon motioned for silence when the innkeeper would announce him. 'She has not yet dined?' Beldon asked in low tones, noting the lack of dinner items.

The innkeeper shook his head. 'She has not been here long and she was wet clear through, the poor dear. She said there'd been a carriage accident, a broken axle or some such.' The innkeeper looked at him sharply, suddenly curious. A husband should know these things. Why hadn't he been travelling with his wife?

Beldon improvised quickly. 'Yes, she was on her way home from visiting her sister. One of her outriders sent word to me to meet her here since the accident prevented her from journeying further.' Lies were tricky things.

'Dinner for two would be in order, the best of what you have, and a bottle of wine.' Beldon suppressed a smile at how quickly the innkeeper was placated. Dinner for two in a private parlour was far more lucrative than one woman alone who was taking her time before ordering. Beldon pressed some money into the man's hand and sent him away.

Beldon studied her briefly in silence. Her back

was to him, her travelling cloak spread before the fire along with a set of clothes. Her toes were balanced on the fender, lapping up the warmth while her half-boots dried. But there was no mistaking the alertness of her body—she was not asleep nor was she relaxed.

All about her were signs that his Lilya was an incredible woman. She had smartly engineered an escape in short order and had clung to the fortitude needed to see it through. Travelling the Cornish roads in poor weather was no mean feat even if she'd managed a ride with a passing wagon. That the escape was from him did not sit well, but he could still admire her.

A beautiful, resourceful woman was rare indeed. She was probably armed as well as resourceful, Beldon reminded himself. He had no desire to end up skewered with one of her throwing knives.

He coughed discreetly at the doorway before moving forwards. 'Lilya.'

She started at the sound, a hand instinctively reaching for the knife at her calf, her body in a smooth half-crouch before he could clarify.

'It's me, Lilya.' He swiftly removed his hat, showing her all of his face.

Her posture relaxed. But she did not throw herself into his arms, did not run to him in relief the way she'd turned to him today in the stable yard. 'You're not supposed to be here.'

Beldon forced a smile. 'That's hardly a warm welcome. I've braved the Cornish roads and most of the inns between here and Pendennys for you.' He shrugged out of his wet things and made himself at home, keeping a firm rein on the emotions simmering beneath his casual façade. Anger warred with relief. He'd found her, but how dare she think she could leave him, even if her sentiments were of the noblest degree.

Dinner arrived, a delicious roast with carrots and potatoes, and a rich red wine. Beldon poured the wine and held out a chair for her by the fire as if nothing were wrong. 'Come and eat, you will need your strength and we have much to talk about.'

Beldon was furious. His show of nonchalance did not fool her for a moment. Lilya tentatively took the seat he offered. She had seen him angry before. He'd been angry the night he'd caught Christoph stealing a kiss in the garden. But she'd not ever seen him like this, feral power without even the veneer of manners to dull its potency. Had such power always been there, effectively subdued into something more socially manageable? It was hard to imagine that the gentleman who waltzed divinely was also capable of such primal reactions. One automatically assumed a polished gentleman of Beldon Stratten's calibre had had such base instincts bred out of him. But such an assumption was clearly false. It made him all the more attractive to her and her pulse quickened at the prospect.

It occurred to her as well as she pushed her meat about her plate, waiting for the other proverbial shoe to fall, that his assumptions about her were perhaps flawed, too. Constrained by society's looking glass, perhaps he struggled to see beyond her fragile beauty, struggled to see the strength within. He knew she was no wilting violet. He had witnessed proof on several occasions, but still had not accepted it. What kind of shrinking female carried a knife and used it with accuracy?

Lilya set down her fork. It was time to deal with those assumptions. 'I have to leave. You know this. No one is safe while I am here. We were fooling ourselves.' But what a pity to leave now, when there was so much more to Beldon Stratten to discover.

'A few weeks, Lilya?' Beldon put down his own fork and folded his arms across his chest, eyes blazing. 'A few weeks was all it took for a man to rip asunder what God had joined together? You would abandon your husband?'

The words shamed her. Her anger flared. Did he really not understand the reason she fled? 'It is out of devotion that I leave you. I will not see you dead. In the end, your title cannot protect me or you. We had hoped it would. Today proved we were wrong.' Oh, how she'd wanted to believe such protection was possible. But words were only words, titles or not. They were not shields for the reality that hunted her.

Beldon nodded, his eyes hard jewels that intently studied her. 'And the "in sickness and in health" part? "In good times and bad? For richer or poorer?"' he challenged. 'Did those mean nothing to you as well?' He paused and said slowly, 'Or did you think they meant nothing to me? Is that it, Lilya? Do you doubt me?'

'You were raised a gentleman from birth and taught a gentleman's code without ever truly choosing it for yourself. You do what is "right" without questioning it. You champion me because a gentleman should. You did not seek this marriage of your own accord. You should not be bound to it.'

Cold fury simmered along the tight muscles of his body; she could visibly see it in the corded strength of his arms. But she would not flinch, she would not give up the table first, although her instincts screamed she should get up and create space between them.

'Lilya, do you love me? You see, I must wonder when you think so little of the characteristics I possess, noble as they are.' His voice sent an icy tremor through her. 'It is a wonder you consented to marry me at all seeing the low esteem in which you hold my code of conduct.'

Is that what he thought? How could he believe for a moment that her desire for him was feigned in any way? How could a body fake such responses? That she would have allowed him access to her body, to her heart, in the most private of ways, only to mislead him?

She rose, unable to remain seated in her agitation.

'There is much you might question, but not that, never that, Beldon.' She shook her head in disbelief that he would even think such a thing.

'How could I not love you? With you, I found all things: passion, a lover, a friend. I had never thought to experience that for myself. How could you even doubt that I love you?'

'You love me, and yet you reject me.'

'Because my love will destroy you, Beldon. Even now you seek to do the gentlemanly thing without realising what it will cost you.'

'And living without you won't? Won't destroy me?' Beldon's voice was a fierce growl. 'You think I married you out of a need to protect, out of a need to fulfil a social obligation because that's what a gentleman does when a damsel is in distress.' His tone softened slightly, his eyes going to the tourmaline bracelet. 'Do you know when I bought that? I sent for it the day after we'd gone to the jewellers'. You see, I'd already decided you were the one, before I bedded you, before Christoph was caught skulking upstairs the night of the reception. I'd already decided.'

'Even more reason to let me leave now, Beldon.

You made that choice before you knew everything. You are sticking to it now out of stubborn pride because a gentleman never goes back on his word,' Lilya cried. Why did he have to make this so difficult? She just wanted to save him—was that so hard to understand?

With a swift movement he grasped her wrist, the bracelet sliding towards her elbow. 'I have only one heart, Lilya. I have given it to you—why is that so hard to accept? Why will you so eagerly throw it away and doom us both to separate lives of misery?'

'You can't have me and Pendennys both. Whoever is looking for me will always start there. Even if Christoph is eliminated, others will come, others will follow his trail and it will always lead there, it will always lead home.' The home he loved would become a prison for them both and it would slowly deteriorate.

Five heartbeats spanned the silence.

'I know.'

She was not ready for his answer. She'd expected him to argue, the old, tired and now patently false arguments of protection, that no one dared to hurt a peer of the realm. But she had not expected this. The answer was admittance, but it was not a defeat.

Beldon dropped her wrist and strode to the door, locking it with a resounding click.

'What are you doing?' Lilya queried, watching

this potent man advance on her, desire rising as his hands went to the buttons of his damp shirt.

'I am going to make love to my wife; afterwards, we're going to plan our future.' He seized her about the waist and ravaged her mouth with a kiss, but she recognised at once his anger was gone, replaced by something else more primal and just as fierce. There'd be none of the gentleman in this coupling tonight and her body welcomed it. He pushed her back to the table, her buttocks meeting the hard wood, his hands shoving up her skirts, both of them breathing hard with their arousal.

'The dishes,' she managed between savage kisses.

'Damn,' came the muttered expletive. Beldon turned her away from him, his erection hard against the bunched folds of her skirt. He had her skirts fully pushed up to her waist in a moment, the warm air of the room a teasing caress on her bared skin, his intentions clear. He meant to take her from behind the way a stallion takes his mare. A forbidden thrill coursed through her as she braced her arms on the table. Beldon's arm was about her waist, steadying her, supporting her against the onslaught of his body. She felt the nudge of his manhood against her, then she took all of him, revelling in the force of her lover's prowess until her cries could not be contained and he spilled himself in her, pumping his seed to the very core of her being.

They stayed that way for a while, with him locked

inside of her, her body pressed against the warmth of his, both breathing hard. Lilya recognised through the mists of her passion that something extraordinary had happened. This had been a coupling of both body and mind. Here, amid the roughness of their loving, they had seen each other plain, perhaps for the first time, both of them naked beyond the literal sense. The gentleman and the delicate débutante had been set aside so that a man and a woman could take their place. She wanted that man beyond all reason and he wanted that woman. For now that was enough.

Recovered, Beldon made a bed of sorts for them on the floor with their dried cloaks. She rested her head against Beldon's shoulder in the firelight, overcome with a new satisfaction.

Beldon's hand gently stroked through her hair, idly combing it with his fingers. 'Do you have everything with you? Is there anything back at the house that you need?'

'No,' she answered. She meant it, too. In a matter of hours, the world had become infinitely simpler. The wardrobes of gowns had been replaced by two serviceable carriage dresses and a single pair of boots, her father's legacy and a few pocket-sized personal items.

Beldon nodded, his profile limned in the firelight to reveal the proud bones of his face. 'Good, then we are ready to die for our love.'

'As I am sure you're aware, you'll have to explain

that statement.' Lilya sat up, shaking her hair back from her face. What did he intend?

There before the fire, Beldon outlined a simple plan, made no less extraordinary for its simplicity, but perhaps the more so by it. 'We head to Roseland and then take a ship. Once on board, we send out word that we've been lost at sea,' he began. 'We will have simply disappeared. We'll be at the bottom of the ocean along with the diamond.'

'And what then? When we're "dead", I mean?'

'Then we can go anywhere we like, as long as it isn't England. We could go to South America, I have mining interests there in the British holdings in the Argentine and there's quite a Cornish population there. We could go to America and run a horse farm. The options are endless even within our limited parameters.'

It went without saying that parts of the world were definitely off limits. They could not risk going east to the Continent or staying in the British Isles. The enormity of his plan was not lost on her.

'What of Pendennys? We cannot be convenient ghosts.'

'I have named young Alexander the heir. He will inherit and, until he comes of age, Valerian will be my custodian.'

It was as it should be, no one would find fault with that. Baby Alex was his closest male relative. Valerian would be a legitimate trustee for the estate until then. Pendennys would not suffer. But Beldon? She reached for his hand. He was giving up more than a title for her.

'I know what Pendennys means to you.'

'And I know what you mean to me,' Beldon replied.

What she'd always meant to him. She could see that this was not a hastily concocted plan. For all its simplicity, the believability of it required forethought and detail. He'd been planning this for a while. He had to have been to have a will, to have decided that he would walk away from Pendennys. For her. And in true Beldon fashion, it was all orchestrated for efficiency. He had thought of everyone's needs. No loose ends were left untied.

'Do you have the papers with you?' She was curious to know just how organised he'd been.

'Yes.'

The single word overwhelmed her. In the rain, in the dark, after having his estate threatened, he'd thrown on a cloak, mounted his horse and simply rode away with his future tucked in his pocket to follow her.

'Incredible,' she breathed. 'Absolutely incredible.'

Chapter Twenty

Christoph had come to the conclusion over coffee in the morning that the baron was either incredibly stupid or incredibly canny. Last night's torrential rain would have stopped any sane man from further adventures and maybe it had stopped the baron. Pendennys had left last night and not come back.

There were lots of reasons the baron hadn't come back. Most of them had to do with the realities of the weather. Darkness was hard enough to travel in without the mud-drenched roads. He'd probably holed up in an inn somewhere to wait out the storm. There were countless inns and small towns up and down the coast. It was impossible to know how far he'd gone and where he'd stopped. Chances were he'd be back in the morning.

Of course the man would be back in the morning. The alternative was ridiculous in the extreme. What man rode away from his estate with nothing more but a horse and his riding gear? And yet that very thought niggled at Christoph Agyros. The only thing he knew for certain was that Pendennys had ridden out looking for his wife. That made two of them who didn't know where Lilya had gone.

While he'd waited and watched, Lilya had slipped past him. This was worrisome. He had no idea where Lilya had gone. She could have gone to either Fowey or Falmouth, one north, one south. But the baron had headed towards Falmouth, Christoph had verified it before he'd been pushed off the road by bad weather.

It was crucial he find Pendennys. If Lilya wasn't with him already, Pendennys was the only link to her. Christoph hoped to catch him on the road home from Falmouth, ideally dragging his wife behind him. But time and again, Pendennys had proved himself to be more than the usual man. He'd travelled with a fresh bullet wound, refusing to succumb to fever like any normal man. He'd even married Lilya Stefanov, *knowing* the enormous troubles that came with her.

Pendennys had not acted like any usual man then, why would he do so now? The moment Christoph finished eating, he'd get back out there and start searching the Falmouth road. Capturing Pendennys would be a start and a sure lure to bring Lilya out of hiding. She'd never let her husband suffer for her. The plan was simple enough.

* * *

Simple plans were not without their hitches, Beldon reflected the next morning. He stood at the window of the inn's best chamber in the morning light, dressed only in his undergarments. He let the rosy sunrise fall across his body, savouring the newness of the day, his eyes closed, his thoughts turned inward to what this new day would bring: a new start, a new life. If all went well, by the end of the day he'd no longer be Baron Pendennys. Baron Pendennys and his new bride would have died in a tragic accident along the coastal road. But Mr Matthew Glenhurst and his wife, Catherine, would be setting out on their new life together aboard a ship bound for Ireland and then America.

Beldon stretched from side to side, going through his usual routine of morning exercises. If all went well… That was the key. It was one thing to plan a disappearance. It was another to actually pull it off.

Timing would be everything. They'd have to stay around town and let themselves be seen this morning. He wanted people running some errands. But he did not want to wait too long in Falmouth in case Christoph had worked out they were not at Pendennys.

Regardless, he'd have to wait long enough for the shops to open and to reach the bank. He wanted his money before his 'demise' later in the day. He had funds in London, too, but he'd need Valerian to privately make those accessible to him later.

Beldon stretched out on the cold floor to work his abdomen with a series of exercises. It was laughable really, all his plans. Not one of them had come to fruition. They'd all been derailed or reshaped in some fashion. He'd gone to London with a list of wifely attributes, only to discard them in favour of Lilya. He'd planned for an evacuation of Pendennys if necessary. Supplies had been laid in, a carriage readied so that they could flee in comfort, well provisioned. Instead, he'd ridden out of Pendennys with pistols, the clothes on his back, a roll of pound notes and a set of papers tucked into his cloak.

Now, he was 'planning' the next phase of their escape, but who knew how it would turn out?

In the bed, Lilya stirred among the sheets and Beldon stopped his exercises to watch her slumber, her hair tumbled about her on the pillow. She'd slept well after he'd carried her upstairs, as had he. The previous day had been tiring, but he thought the quality of sleep was from something more than sheer exhaustion. They'd reached a new level of understanding downstairs last night, not only of each other, but of themselves.

It had taken the stripping away of all the trappings of their life to comprehend what they truly meant to each other. Pendennys was his life, or so he'd thought, right up until last night. When he'd returned to find Lilya gone, it had been far easier than he would have believed to simply walk out the door to find her. Only he hadn't walked, he had raced, because Lilya was out there and Christoph was out there and Heaven forbid Christoph find her first. Even in the morning light and the sanity that was reputed to return with the dawn, he knew he'd chosen well. Lilya was all that mattered. He wanted to live in freedom with her, wherever that was.

The things she'd professed last night still overwhelmed him. She'd been willing to give up her personal happiness in order to save him, willing to simply disappear to free him. It was extraordinary, really, to be loved so thoroughly, although the consequences could have been dire. Life without Lilya would be a half-life at best.

He crawled back into bed, the warmth of her body taking the chill off the morning, and kissed her gently. 'Time to wake up, my dear, and begin the rest of our lives.'

'Mmmm,' Lilya murmured, sniffing the air. 'Love and bacon, that sounds very promising. I could get used to that.'

Beldon laughed, rolling her beneath him. 'I sincerely hope you do.' The rest of their lives was getting off to a good start.

The morning passed uneventfully. The rain that had impeded him yesterday was an ally today. The summer storm had passed in the night, leaving the

roads soft in places with mud that had not yet hard-
ened. Travel would be slow not only for him and
Lilya, but for Christoph, too. For those reasons,
Beldon was eager to be off. The more distance he
could put between himself and Christoph, the better.

Beldon had them underway by half past ten. He
was mounted on his stallion and Lilya on a rented
gelding with a sturdy temperament, her clothing
packed in a valise from the innkeeper. Taking a gig
was out of the question. They'd spend the better part
of the day pushing a gig out of ruts.

Lilya was nervous; he could feel the tension
radiating from her body when he gave her a leg up.
'Don't worry,' he whispered, swinging up behind
her. 'It's a beautiful day for a ride and at the end of
it we'll be at Val's.' Nature *had* given them a lovely
day in exchange for the drenching night. The sky
was blue overhead and it promised to be pleasantly
warm later in the day. Everything would be fine as
long as they didn't have to race anywhere.

'We won't outrun anyone.' Lilya gave voice to
the most obvious concern, but the odds were in their
favour.

'Christoph can't give chase any faster than we can
go with the roads in this shape,' Beldon reassured
her confidently. He guided his horse on to the road
and into the light stream of traffic exiting Falmouth.

'Unless he's waiting up ahead.' Lilya's eyes darted

from side to side, searching for a likely spot for an ambush.

'He would have to be very sure of himself to take that chance,' Beldon countered. 'He'd have to know without doubt we'd gone to Falmouth and not Fowey. His luck has been a little thin on the ground by my count. I don't think he'll be feeling lucky enough to stake that kind of claim.' But for good measure, Beldon's hand closed over the butt of the pistol beneath his riding cloak.

Forewarned was forearmed. If Christoph's luck hadn't been good, his own had not been much better. If Christoph knew neither of them were at Pendennys by now, it would be safe to assume the chase was engaged. He was out there somewhere.

By mid-afternoon, the weather had changed again, clouds blowing in from the ocean, the sun obscured behind them. A fat raindrop hit their faces two miles from Roseland. Beside him, Lilya pulled up the hood of her cloak, casting a pessimistic glance at the ominous sky. The trip had taken twice its usual time with the slow roads and the mud sucking at the horses' hooves.

Beldon squinted into the distance. Damn. Another delay. The road appeared to be blocked by trees that had fallen during the night. Damn and double damn. This part of the road to Roseland was not well populated. He'd turned off the main road a little way back in order to take a more direct route to Valerian's. He'd have to move the trees on his own without the benefit of help from others on the road. He hoped his shoulder was up for it. It would have to be unless they wanted to walk the last two miles.

The unblocked margin between the road and cliff edge was fairly narrow. The edge was dangerously soft, a mudslide waiting to happen. Beldon reined his stallion to a halt and hopped down to survey the damage.

He kicked a booted foot at the tree trunks. They'd fallen in a slant across the road. If he could trust the ground on the other side and if he had been alone, he'd have jumped Randolph over them. There was no chance of getting Lilya's rented gelding over them. The horse was stocky and built for endurance, not for jumping. Beldon tested one of the tree trunks, but it was too heavy for a single man to move. Even if his shoulder had been in good health, it would have been impossible.

He stood there, hands on hips, his mind going through his list of options. The list was short. There was only one. Lead the horses around on the narrow bit of path between the cliff and the road.

'I'll take Randolph first and then come back for your horse.'

'I can lead my horse, he seems docile enough,' Lilya offered, not wanting to be left behind.

Beldon cast an assessing glance at the narrow strip

of land and shook his head. 'I don't want to risk too much weight at once on the ground. We don't know how strong the cliff edge is. Or if your horse spooks for any reason, we don't all want to be out on that strip.' He didn't mean to lose Lilya to a mudslide just when he'd discovered how much she meant to him.

'I'll be right back, my dear,' Beldon reassured her with a quick kiss.

He grabbed Randolph's reins with as much good cheer as he could summon up and began the dangerous trek around the edge. The distance comprised perhaps a hundred yards, but it was every bit as treacherous as he'd feared. The ground was soft and it took all his strength to keep Randolph pressed to the side away from the lip of the edge where the ground was at its softest. There was only one perilous slip where the ground had threatened to give out. Randolph had balked, sensing the danger, but low soothing words had got him through it.

Beldon looked back at the path, now marked with hoofprints and boots. He opted to climb over the tree trunks for his return. The path was every bit as slippery as he'd predicted. The fewer pressures on it, the better. He'd climb over and get Lilya's horse and tell Lilya to start climbing through. He would not risk her out on that rim after two horses had passed.

Beldon took the tree trunks agilely, calling out as he went, 'Lilya, I'm coming over the top.'

'Stay where you are, Pendennys,' came the cold male response. That was not Lilya's voice.

Beldon crested the trunks, horror freezing him. Christoph stood there, holding Lilya and a gun. Lilya was pale, her face stoically blank. 'I will shoot her, Pendennys.'

'Then I will shoot you. You don't think I am unarmed, do you?' Beldon ground out, his mind flying over options, of which there were none. With Lilya pressed to him, Christoph could not be rushed. Beldon could not launch himself at Christoph without also landing on Lilya and there was no guarantee she'd be safe from a random gunshot if the gun misfired.

There was another consideration, too. Christoph didn't look right. This was not the man who'd so suavely presented himself in London's ballrooms with the manners of a gentleman. It wasn't that he was dirty from travel or merely tired. It was his eyes. They looked feverish, mad almost. A man who'd become unhinged was not a logical creature. Beldon must tread carefully here.

'All right,' Beldon said slowly. 'What do you want?'

'I want the diamond. I know she has it.'

Beldon shook his head. 'I know nothing of a diamond. She does not have whatever it is you're looking for. Let her go and take your obsession with my wife elsewhere.'

'You lie!' Christoph exploded, shoving Lilya away from him in a quick, jerky move that caused her to fall. 'Let's try it this way.' The gun shifted to him. 'Lilya, you'll be more inclined to co-operate,' he sneered. 'Give me the diamond or I'll shoot your husband.'

'So you can shoot me moments later?' Lilya picked herself up off the ground slowly and Beldon thought she might have slid a hand beneath her skirt. *Don't do it, Lilya*, he thought silently. Don't go after that madman with your knife. Beldon was helpless up on the tree trunks. Leaping on Christoph now would only result in acquiring a gaping chest wound.

'I would take you with me, Lilya. You could be my wife and we could rule Greece together.' The man had truly lost his mind. He made a wild gesture with the gun. 'Hurry now, Lilya, make up your mind.'

Beldon could see her falter, unsure what to do.

'I've already had him shot once. This time I won't miss,' Christoph taunted her.

Lilya seemed to come to some sort of decision. 'All right. But Beldon has to get the diamond. It's in the saddle bag on his horse.' Beldon stifled a groan. It was to be an exchange, then.

'You for the diamond,' Christoph growled at Lilya, 'on the path over there.'

With that, Beldon hastily retreated and rummaged the saddle bag until he found what he was looking for, a black velvet pouch. Then he went to his end of the trail, his heart racing. Surely the trail would hold under Lilya's weight. Surely Christoph was mad enough to claim his prize and go. No, none of it was sure. It was all very frightening. Beldon had one hand around the black pouch and the other around his pistol. He'd fire if he had the chance. He'd do whatever it took to free his wife of Christoph Agyros.

Lilya stepped out on to the path, her eyes holding his, trying so very hard not to look down, trying not to be afraid. When she was halfway, at the most perilous part of the trail, Agyros yelled, 'Toss her the bag, Pendennys. Then she can toss it to me.'

Beldon shook his head. 'No, I'll toss her the bag, but she leaves it there. You can come out and get it.' Otherwise, he had no guarantee Agyros wouldn't shoot Lilya after he had the jewel.

Lilya gasped, drawing his attention. She took a jiggy little side step as dirt loosened and slid where she stood.

Beldon tossed Lilya the bag. Time was running out. He knew just how exposed the land was. He wasn't risking her. 'Put the bag down, Lilya, and move towards me, slowly,' he ordered. 'If you try anything, Agyros, I'll have a bullet in you.'

Lilya caught the bag and bent to set it down. 'No, show me the diamond first,' Agyros protested. 'There could be anything in that bag.'

Lilya straightened and pulled the gem out, holding it up between her thumb and forefinger. An unholy light lit Agyros's eyes. She slid it back into the bag, but Agyros was a man possessed and he did not wait. He leapt at Lilya, his move pushing them both off balance and teetering near the cliff edge. 'Lilya!' Beldon launched himself towards the madman with no care for his own safety, but his efforts were too late. There was the briefest of warning and then the ground collapsed beneath them and they all began a long tumbling slide to the bottom of the cliff.

Beldon hit the ground hard, aware that he was barely conscious. Breathing was becoming painfully impossible and his thoughts were scattered. With the last vestiges of consciousness, he struggled upwards against the mud that sought to trap him. He could not die here. He had to find Lilya. Where was she? Where was Christoph? But he had no answers as the darkness claimed him.

Where was the diamond? The thought roused Christoph to action. He did not care how long he'd lain there or if he'd been unconscious. He cared only that his quarry lay on the shale beach, somewhere. The aches of his body were nothing compared to the prize if he could get up and move. He'd seen it! The diamond was more beautiful than he'd imagined.

He levered himself upright with the help of a large boulder. He was horribly filthy, covered in mud, his clothes in tatters. Never mind that the mud had probably saved his life. A harder landing would have seen him with a broken leg, if not worse. Christoph breathed hard against the simple exertion of walking, the uneven ground of the shale beach complicating his limping gait. With luck, Pendennys had perished somewhere nearby. But he was not interested in Pendennys at the moment. He wanted to find Lilya and when he did he'd take the diamond from her.

Malicious images filled his mind at the thought of retrieving the diamond. The bag had still been in her hand when the cliff had collapsed. He'd take the diamond and then he'd make her pay. He'd strip that bitch piece by piece of her clothing, of her dignity, making her suffer until the diamond had nothing left to hide behind. Then, if it behooved her sensibilities, she could crawl naked to the road. No less than she deserved for the troubles she'd put him through.

A dark shape lay close by. He hobbled towards it. Lilya! He was greedy in his reward. She was not conscious. Perhaps she was already dead. His revenge would be diminished, but his retrieval would be efficient. His ankle pained him, making balance and walking difficult. He straddled her, carefully steadying himself to stay upright as he searched for the diamond. There it was, the bag lay in her hand, her fist tight around it. Victory at last. All he had to do was reach out and take it.

Chapter Twenty-One

W here was Lilya? Beldon did not know how long he'd lain there, only that it was nearly dark around him now and he'd no doubt been unconscious for a while. Every bone ached, each movement a painful experience, but miraculously he didn't feel anything was broken, just extremely sore and bruised. He knew only one thing: he had to move. He had to find Lilya. He'd pieced his thoughts together. The ground had given way beneath them. All of them had fallen.

In the fading light, if he was careful, Beldon could lift his head and see the slope they'd slid down. He dared to push himself into a sitting position.

Debris from the slide was all about him. Fear gave him strength. Where was Lilya? Beldon got to his knees, crawling across the rocks, panic seizing him.

A glimpse of white against the dimming light drew his attention. He looked again. The white had moved. Perhaps the white of a man's shirt? Focusing his gaze, Beldon could see it was a shape, half-crawling, half-stumbling towards something. A man— Christoph! Who else would be down here?

The man crouched over the still shape, a depraved laugh reaching Beldon's ears. Lilya! Beldon pushed to his feet, stumbling, rushing the short distance, a hoarse roar on his lips. Christoph turned too slowly to meet his onslaught. Beldon staggered into him with the force of an enraged bull. How dare the man lay hands on his wife! Beldon took him backwards, away from Lilya's prone form.

Agyros was in no better shape than he, and Agyros toppled easily in his surprise. But he had a strength born of madness and a knife to go with it. He scrambled away from Beldon, taking to his feet in an ungainly lurch. His clothes were ripped, his face dirty with mud, all veneer of the gentleman he proclaimed to be stripped away. His knife glinted dully in the fading light, a threatening menace.

'Leave her be. It's me you want.' It was a bold lie with only a grain of truth. It was not revenge against Beldon that had driven Agyros to the brink of insanity. It was the diamond. He wanted nothing more than the diamond.

Beldon gestured for him to come on, leading him away from Lilya. Oh God, why didn't she move? 'I've bested you from the beginning, Agyros. Last time pays for all—come, try your luck again against a real man. Even a coward can overcome an unconscious woman.'

His taunts worked; Agyros stumbled towards him. Beldon's eyes watched the knife hand. He would make Agyros come to him, make Agyros attack. If he fell, he doubted he'd get up with ease. He'd be too vulnerable on the ground and he wanted this done quickly.

Christoph's eyes gave him away a moment before he struck. Beldon let him come, side-stepping clumsily at the last, Christoph's knife meeting only air. Christoph's balance faltered, he stumbled, unprepared for the lack of impact, and fell.

Beldon leapt forwards as best he could, ready to finish the fight, the heat of battle upon him. But the battle was already finished. Christoph Agyros lay unmoving on the shale shards of the rocks where his head had taken a fatal blow. Later, Beldon would appreciate what Christoph's death meant: the war for the diamond was over for now. But he had little time to savour that victory. All his concern was riveted on returning to Lilya.

True exhaustion threatened to claim him. The aches of his body returned with the ebbing of adrenalin. Sleep, unconsciousness tugged at him. Beldon fought it. He could not succumb yet. Lilya needed him.

Beldon crawled to her side. She was pale.

Deathly so. Beldon held a hand to her lips, searching for a tell-tale sign of breath. *Please, please, please.* Today was supposed to be the start of their lives. Not the end.

There! His heart raced. He felt it again. There was breath against his hand, faint though it was. 'Lilya.' He called her name, running his hands over her body, searching for signs of ruin. She moaned. Ribs, he thought. Bruised or broken. He hoped not broken. A broken rib posed all nature of dangers, not the least being a punctured lung. Beldon shut his eyes, willing away that particular disaster.

Lilya shivered. Beldon gathered her to him, satisfied she could be moved at least that far without causing more damage. Perhaps his warmth would rouse her. He didn't know what else to do, what else he *could* do. His own strength was fading rapidly, his reserves dwindling to nothing. If he slept, it might very well be the end of them both. How long would they survive, mangled and cold at the bottom of a cliff? No one knew where they were.

It was bitter consolation to know his plan had worked all too well. He'd meant to have them 'die', although not literally. Why now with Christoph defeated? The diamond safe? It was the cruellest of ironies that their escape was ensured, but they were powerless to take it.

Beldon blinked hard against sleep. He could not give in. But one could only fight the inevitable for so long. Perhaps there were worse ways to die, he thought, slipping slowly towards oblivion, his arms tight about Lilya. After all, he'd die with the woman he loved in his arms and her enemy defeated.

Wait. Were those lantern lights at the top of the cliff? It was quite possible his eyes were playing tricks on him. There they were again. Beldon knew the lights wouldn't pick them up. He and Lilya were tucked too far back unless one looked directly over the cliff. He had to get himself out where the light would pick him up. But that meant leaving Lilya.

It was time for the last decision. With the very last of his strength, Beldon crawled out on to the beach, clinging to one desperate hope. Val. Somehow Val had known to come.

Valerian ranged the cliff road like a black lion, his cloak whipping about his boot tops in the wind. Where was Beldon? His gamekeeper had picked up the stallion running loose on the estate's perimeter late that afternoon. That in itself was curious. What would Beldon's stallion be doing so far from home unless Beldon had ridden him? Their estates were on opposite sides of Falmouth, a two-hour ride apart. But Valerian had the note from Beldon's messenger and he knew danger was afoot. Had Beldon ridden out and met with foul play on the road?

Philippa had been frantic with worry over her brother and he'd set out immediately in the hopes of putting her fears to rest—his fears, too. Surrounded by outriders carrying lanterns and guns, Valerian had combed the cliff road leading from Falmouth to Roseland to no avail. His frustration grew at the sight of the roadblock ahead. It would take daylight and the work of many men to remove the trees in the road. If Beldon had fallen into trouble on the other side, he would have no way of knowing. Waiting until daylight would be waiting too long.

It appeared Randolph had jumped. Horse hooves picked up on this side of the barrier. It would have been one hell of a jump, even for Beldon's magnificent hunter, but not impossible. There seemed to be no alternative. The road had given way on the edge. It didn't seem likely the horse had gone around. Unless…unless the road had been there and then collapsed. That alternative was unthinkable.

'Milord, there's something you should see.' One of the outriders gestured to the edge of the cliff where his other men were gathered.

Valerian saw immediately what had garnered their attention. The slim thread of road not blocked by the trees had been washed away on their side. Valerian knelt, his keen eyes taking in road beyond the trees, the other side of the barricade.

'Shine a lantern over there,' he commanded. 'I see tracks. Anyone care to verify?' A second set of eyes verified his supposition. Valerian's tracker's mind went into action. The mud had dried, preserving the signs of hoof prints that went right up to the barrier and stopped. There were other signs, too. 'We need to hoist a man over the trees. I think there's more than one set of tracks.'

After a long set of minutes, the man clambered back over the trees. 'You're right, milord, there's three sets of horse hooves over there. Looked as if some of the horses might have been racing from the spacing of their steps.

Valerian nodded, a horrifying scenario taking shape. Beldon had Lilya and, in light of the message, they were on the run, attempting to elude Christoph. But the road had been blocked and they found themselves chased to a dead end.

Beldon would have fought to the last. He knew his friend. Beldon would have tried the narrow path that had existed before the mudslide. Val knelt at the cliff's edge and peered down, half-hoping, half-praying he wouldn't find proof of his hypothesis.

'Shine as many lights as you can down there. It appears there was a mudslide,' Val said grimly. A moment later he rocked back on his heels. Oh God. There was a man lying at an awkward angle.

A man whistled. 'That's one heck of a fall, milord. There won't be any survivors.'

No, it was not possible that his friend would have perished, pushed to reckless chances by Christoph and his gang. 'Bring the rope,' Valerian ordered. 'I'll tie it about my waist and make my way down the

slide. If there are any survivors they'll need our help.'
If not, he thought privately, he would bring the bodies
home for Philippa and Constantine.

Bright lights pierced Beldon's eyelids. He was
supposed to be dead. Was this the afterlife? It needed
curtains.

'Beldon?'

He must have groaned out loud. He forced his
eyes open. Philippa was there, standing over him,
and, thank goodness, blocking out the light. Someone moved near his feet.

'He's awake.' Philippa was talking to someone.
Her hand went to his brow. 'No fever.'

'Good.' Weight shoved off the bed and Valerian
came to stand beside Philippa. Val looked terrible.
Dark circles dominated his face.

'I'm not dead?' Beldon queried.

Philippa smiled. 'No, you're quite alive.'

Then he remembered his joy over the fact was
conditional. He scanned their faces. 'And Lilya?'

Philippa reached for his hand and he knew a
moment's panic. 'She's fine. She's resting in the next
room.'

'She's awake?'

'She's just had breakfast.' Val put a restraining hand on his chest. 'Her ribs are bound, but not
broken. You're both lucky. If it had been winter, you
wouldn't have survived the elements. As it was, the

unseasonably cold summer damp did you no favours. I want to know what happened.'

'Christoph came after us,' Beldon explained. Philippa fluffed his pillows and Valerian insisted on helping him sit up when he tried to do it on his own. Once settled to their satisfaction, Beldon launched into the tale, starting with the disaster at Pendennys and ending with the wild encounter on the road to Roseland.

'It is as I expected, then.' Val nodded when he finished. 'Christoph is dead.'

'I know. Christoph and I fought after the fall. He was…' The horrible images of Christoph over Lilya were too strongly etched for him to articulate them comfortably. His voice broke. 'I had to defend Lilya.'

'You don't need to say more,' Val assured him. 'You're both safe now. Everyone can celebrate the fact that you're alive.'

'For a while,' Beldon said cautiously. 'That's why we were on our way here.'

'Whatever are you talking about?' Philippa looked aghast, but already her mind was grasping the concept and its consequences.

'Sit down, I'll tell you. Val, get my cloak, the papers are in there.

'There will be others who will come looking for the diamond. Our only chance is to convince all interested parties that the diamond has been lost to history. I mean for us to be lost at sea. When Lilya and I die at sea and her body is committed to the deep, the diamond is lost, too. It's not as crazy as it sounds.' Beldon shrugged. 'It will fall to you, Val, to spread the word of our demise.'

'It means you can't go home again. You'll be giving up Pendennys,' Philippa said quietly. Beldon heard the unspoken message—*you'll be giving us up.*

He reached for his sister's hand. For so long, they'd been all each other had. 'It's harder to do than you know, but Lilya will never be safe here, I see that now. I can't doom her to a life of constant fear. I love her too much for that.'

'As rightly you should, dear brother.' Philippa's eyes watered. 'Oh dear, I'm such a watering pot when I'm…' She paused, gathering her voice around her tears. 'When I'm expecting.'

Beldon understood. He would not see this baby. He would not stand in the church at St Just beside Valerian for the baptism as he had stood there for young Alexander. All the dreams he'd dreamed of young cousins romping the fields of Pendennys would not come to fruition.

Valerian looked up from the papers he'd opened. 'You've been planning this for a while,' he said quietly, passing the papers to Philippa. 'He's named Alex heir. Pendennys will stay in the family.'

'Does Lilya know?'

'Yes. We fought over it. She wanted to leave. She

wanted to set me free.' Beldon glanced at Valerian. 'I don't know how you managed for nine years. I couldn't even last an hour. When I discovered Lilya was gone, I simply walked out the door after her. I had thought it would be difficult to leave Pendennys when the time came. I had set aside provisions, made lists of instructions. But when the moment came, they didn't matter. Only Lilya mattered.'

Val took the papers from Philippa and folded them. 'Now, let me help you up so you can go to Lilya.'

In the end, they had only a short time to prepare for their next journey and say their farewells. It had been tempting to linger at Roseland, but there were already rumours of concern that Pendennys and his wife had disappeared during the recent storm. They needed to take advantage of that. Val put about the story Beldon had been called away on business.

Perhaps short farewells would be better in any case. A few days later when Lilya could travel, a private boat waited at a quiet cove not far from Roseland to carry them to Ireland, where they would take passage across the Atlantic.

The small group stood at the quay, the boat bobbing at the ready. There was nothing left to do but final farewells. Valerian asked for the fifth time if he had enough money.

Beldon gripped his friend's shoulder with affection. 'Yes, for the last time, yes. I have plenty of money.'

'This is not the life we planned.' Val's throat worked furiously.

Beldon laughed. 'I've learned a few things about plans, Val. They're not all they're cracked up to be.' He glanced over at Lilya and reached for her hand. 'If I'd followed my plans, I'd have missed love.' He winked at Val. 'I have it on good authority that love is one of life's greatest pleasures. The only pleasure, really.'

Val nodded and embraced him once, hard. Then Beldon hugged his sister. 'Perhaps you'll be back some day,' she offered.

'Ghosts can't rise from the grave. But we'll see you again. Perhaps you can come to us, wherever we are.' It was the closest to consolation he could give her. Who knew? In the future it might be possible. He was done with plans for now. The goodbyes were settled.

Beldon helped Lilya aboard. She was crying openly and he held her to him as the boat cast off. She would be all right. *They* would be all right. They had all they needed in each other.

By implicit consent, they stayed at the rail, watching England fade behind them. Ireland lay before them. A new life lay beyond that. Lilya turned in his arms; the sea breeze had dried her tears and a smile spread on her face as she tilted her head up to look at him.

They'd reached the open sea and England was lost to them. Lilya reached inside her cloak and drew out the velvet bag.

'And so the Phanar Diamond slips out of history, supposedly,' Beldon whispered.

'Not yet.' Lilya tilted her head with a smile. She reached into the bag and pulled out the sparkling gem.

'Are you sure?' Beldon asked, holding her gaze with steady eyes. Actually giving up the diamond had not been part of his plans. He'd never asked her to give it up. He knew what this gesture now must cost her, how much private soul-searching had gone into this act. He also knew what it could give her. It would free her if she chose but he would never require it of her. He loved her without conditions.

'Yes, I am sure.' With that, Lilya cocked her arm and flung the diamond into the sea. It made a splendid sun-shot arc as it flew briefly across the sky and then sank into the water.

'It has no power over me any more. I think it would have made me as mad as Christoph in the end.'

'And your obligations to your family? The Stefanov quest has ended now.'

'And rightly so. Someone should have thrown the diamond into the ocean a long time ago.' The look of peace on her face was unmistakable. A great burden had been lifted from them both. They were free now, both of them, and their family, too. Anything was possible.

Beldon laughed out loud at his good fortune. His affairs were in order, apparently the standard prequisite necessary for a good life or death. It was evidently true. At the age of thirty-two he had had both.

He bent to kiss his wife. 'I think I'm going to like the happy-ever-afterlife very much.'

* * * * *

COMING NEXT MONTH FROM

HARLEQUIN®
HISTORICAL

Available September 27, 2011

- **SNOWFLAKES AND STETSONS**
  by **Jillian Hart, Carol Finch, Cheryl St.John**
  (Western Anthology)

- **INNOCENT COURTESAN TO ADVENTURER'S BRIDE**
  by **Louise Allen**
  (Regency)
  Third in *The Transformation of the Shelley Sisters* trilogy

- **THE CAPTAIN'S FORBIDDEN MISS**
  by **Margaret McPhee**
  (Regency)

- **THE DRAGON AND THE PEARL**
  by **Jeannie Lin**
  (Chinese Tang Dynasty)

REQUEST YOUR FREE BOOKS!

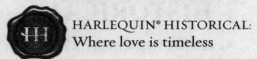

HARLEQUIN® HISTORICAL:
Where love is timeless

2 FREE NOVELS PLUS 2 **FREE GIFTS!**

YES! Please send me 2 FREE Harlequin® Historical novels and my 2 FREE gifts (gifts are worth about $10). After receiving them, if I don't wish to receive any more books, I can return the shipping statement marked "cancel." If I don't cancel, I will receive 6 brand-new novels every month and be billed just $5.19 per book in the U.S. or $5.74 per book in Canada. That's a savings of at least 17% off the cover price! It's quite a bargain! Shipping and handling is just 50¢ per book in the U.S. and 75¢ per book in Canada.* I understand that accepting the 2 free books and gifts places me under no obligation to buy anything. I can always return a shipment and cancel at any time. Even if I never buy another book, the two free books and gifts are mine to keep forever.

246/349 HDN FEQQ

Name _____ (PLEASE PRINT)

Address _____ Apt. #

City _____ State/Prov. _____ Zip/Postal Code

Signature (if under 18, a parent or guardian must sign)

Mail to the **Reader Service:**
IN U.S.A.: P.O. Box 1867, Buffalo, NY 14240-1867
IN CANADA: P.O. Box 609, Fort Erie, Ontario L2A 5X3

Not valid for current subscribers to Harlequin Historical books.

Want to try two free books from another line?
Call 1-800-873-8635 or visit www.ReaderService.com.

* Terms and prices subject to change without notice. Prices do not include applicable taxes. Sales tax applicable in N.Y. Canadian residents will be charged applicable taxes. Offer not valid in Quebec. This offer is limited to one order per household. All orders subject to credit approval. Credit or debit balances in a customer's account(s) may be offset by any other outstanding balance owed by or to the customer. Please allow 4 to 6 weeks for delivery. Offer available while quantities last.

Your Privacy—The Reader Service is committed to protecting your privacy. Our Privacy Policy is available online at www.ReaderService.com or upon request from the Reader Service.

We make a portion of our mailing list available to reputable third parties that offer products we believe may interest you. If you prefer that we not exchange your name with third parties, or if you wish to clarify or modify your communication preferences, please visit us at www.ReaderService.com/consumerschoice or write to us at Reader Service Preference Service, P.O. Box 9062, Buffalo, NY 14269. Include your complete name and address.

HHI1B

Harlequin Romantic Suspense presents the latest book in the scorching new KELLEY LEGACY *miniseries from best-loved veteran series author Carla Cassidy*

Scandal is the name of the game as the Kelley family fights to preserve their legacy, their hearts…and their lives.

Read on for an excerpt from the fourth title
RANCHER UNDER COVER

Available October 2011
from Harlequin Romantic Suspense

"**W**ould you like a drink?" Caitlin asked as she walked to the minibar in the corner of the room. She felt as if she needed to chug a beer or two for courage.

"No, thanks. I'm not much of a drinking man," he replied.

She raised an eyebrow and looked at him curiously as she poured herself a glass of wine. "A ranch hand who doesn't enjoy a drink? I think maybe that's a first."

He smiled easily. "There was a six-month period in my life when I drank too much. I pulled myself out of the bottom of a bottle a little over seven years ago and I've never looked back."

"That's admirable, to know you have a problem and then fix it."

Those broad shoulders of his moved up and down in an easy shrug. "I don't know how admirable it was, all I knew at the time was that I had a choice to make between living and dying and I decided living was definitely more appealing."

She wanted to ask him what had happened preceding that six-month period that had plunged him into the bottom of the bottle, but she didn't want to know too much about him. Personal information might produce a false sense of intimacy that she didn't need, didn't want in her life.

"Please, sit down," she said, and gestured him to the table. She had never felt so on edge, so awkward in her life.

"After you," he replied.

She was aware of his gaze intensely focused on her as she rounded the table and sat in the chair, and she wanted to tell him to stop looking at her as if she were a delectable dessert he intended to savor later.

Watch Caitlin and Rhett's sensual saga unfold amidst the shocking, ripped-from-the-headlines drama of the Kelley Legacy miniseries in

RANCHER UNDER COVER

*Available October 2011
only from Harlequin Romantic Suspense,
wherever books are sold.*

HRSEXP1011

HARLEQUIN® HISTORICAL:
Where love is timeless

Make sure to pick up this Western Christmas
anthology, featuring three delicious
helpings of festive cheer!

Snowflakes and Stetsons

The Cowboy's Christmas Miracle
by Jillian Hart

Unfairly imprisoned, Caleb McGraw thinks nothing can touch him
again. Until he sees his lost son and the caring woman who's
given him a home.

Christmas at Cahill Crossing
by Carol Finch

A growing love for Rosalie Greer persuades ex-Texas Ranger
and loner, Lucas Burnett, to become involved in a special
Cahill Crossing Christmas.

A Magical Gift at Christmas
by Cheryl St.John

Meredith has always dreamed of a grand life but, stranded on a train,
she finds she has everything she needs with just one strong man
to protect her....

Available October 2011.

USA TODAY bestselling author

Carol Marinelli

brings you her new romance

HEART OF THE DESERT

One searing kiss is all it takes for Georgie to know
Sheikh Prince Ibrahim is trouble....

But, trapped in the swirling sands, Georgie finally
surrenders to the brooding rebel prince—yet the
law of his land decrees that she can never
really be his....

Available October 2011.

Available only from Harlequin Presents®.